The Art of Cartography

The Art of Cartography

stories by **J. S. Marcus**

Alfred A. Knopf   New York   1 9 9 1

THIS IS A BORZOI BOOK
PUBLISHED BY ALFRED A. KNOPF, INC.

The author wishes to acknowledge the support of the MacDowell Colony,
the Yaddo Corporation, and the Virginia Center for the Creative Arts.
Several of the stories in this collection were originally published in
Antaeus, GQ, Harper's, The New Yorker, and *The Quarterly.*

Library of Congress Cataloging-in-Publication Data
Marcus, J. S.
The art of cartography : stories / by J.S. Marcus. — 1st ed.
p.   cm.
ISBN 0-394-55946-0
PS3563.A6386A78   1991
813'.54—dc20   90-43243   CIP

Manufactured in the United States of America
FIRST EDITION

For Jack and Isabel Marcus

Along the fine tan sandy shelf
is the land tugging at the sea from under?

ELIZABETH BISHOP

CONTENTS

The Art of Cartography

The Art of Cartography

I read, in several newspapers, about a man from Los Angeles who wanted to go to Oakland. Nothing unusual. A business trip. A family visit. Accounts varied. Some hours later when his plane landed in Auckland, New Zealand, hands went up in the air. The passenger, the airline, the airports, and certain readers considered explanations: Had there been an auditory hallucination? a clerical error? a conspiracy? It's like all those bombs that never seem to go off.

Physically, economically, politically, nobody wants to be in the middle, and everybody wants to be on the edge. The effort made, the money spent, the stance taken; only the furniture remains. People are leaving their homes, their families, their careers, some—like our man in Auckland—without even knowing it. Jaunts to the Horn of Africa. Forays into Eastern Europe. Helicopter drops in South American jungles. A new diaspora.

In London, guests stand at the edge of the room. The man directing our film, a man renowned for his bitterness, bloomed during his month in Belgrade. He toured studios, drank seriously with other directors, wooed young actresses in pidgin Serbo-Croatian. Back in London, with news from the front, he is full of unassailable epigrams: "Once there were alchemists and goldsmiths, and now there are only goldsmiths." He raises a glass of whiskey. "One can no longer create," he says. "One can only refine."

The star of our film, a rock singer from Glasgow, is mumbling about bootleg tapes in Bangkok. A graphic designer who is not connected with our film is trying to play a joke on the other guests by pretending to be an ex-convict. The production assistant goes to make coffee; she is certain all her guests are stone drunk.

Originally I was chosen by the producer to do "a little bit of everything," and I often feel the need to ease tensions—at parties, on the set.

I bring a cup of coffee to the rock star.

I ask the graphic designer about the wallpaper at Reading Gaol.

I begin a flirtatious conversation with a cameraman's little sister. She is in London for a week before spending another week someplace else, and she tells me about a bomb scare in a boutique on the King's Road, a bomb scare in Harrods, a bomb scare in a restaurant. "That's one bomb scare for every day I've been here," she says. I get her a second cup of coffee, and she tries not to stare at the rock star, now lying on the floor with his pants undone.

Our director, more disgusted than usual, says "There used to be alchemists and goldsmiths. Now there are only rock-'n'-roll singers."

And terrorists.

I keep moving to new places for indefinite periods of time. The production company I work for is always changing addresses or toying with bankruptcy, and always feuding with members of the casts and crews. Last week, for instance, our producer and our director stopped speaking to each other. Our director, as famous for his stubbornness as he is for his bitterness, thinks all roads lead to Dubrovnik. He hates England and America, and he hates most everyplace else. London is a hospital ward. New York is a concentration camp. Paris is an open sewer. He wants to shoot on location in Dubrovnik. Our producer, a kind man with a large retinue, made the trip to Dubrovnik, but he and certain members of the retinue came down with dysentery. Our producer is holding a grudge. The Scottish rock star goes on tour in six months. Talks are at a standstill.

We could fire the director, or wait for him to quit, or hold out on principle. Or I could quit, or hold out for more money. But none of us seems to do anything, except wait—at parties, in restaurants, on the telephone.

As an employee of the production company, I know that my professional allegiances are with our producer. As someone who has never been to Dubrovnik, I suppose my personal allegiances are with our director. I have no choice, then, but to wait—in the middle.

Our director has given a party and not invited our producer. A playwright, who is an American expatriate, is standing in the pantry discussing his day: "My day begins with a glass of water and a slice of lemon. Later I have a hard-boiled egg. Before I go to sleep I have another glass of water and, perhaps, another slice of lemon."

The director's wife, an Austrian émigrée, puts on a record called "The Unknown Kurt Weill." She translates a song for the people at the bar. "This is a song

of the Brown Islands. The men are evil and the women
are sick. A lady ape does business there and the fields
are withering from the stench of oil."

A woman with dyed hair comes up to the bar, car-
rying the director's photograph of Samuel Beckett.
"Beckett," she says. "Beckett. Is there a more beautiful word in the English language?"

The other day, in the back seat of a taxi, I found a
gothic romance entitled *Mistaken Intentions*. The
cover showed a man and two women. The first woman
was staring at the man, who was staring at the second
woman, who was standing behind the first. The first
woman seemed to be in love with the man, and probably assumed he was in love with her. But I was certain he wasn't. He was looking affectionately at the
second woman, who seemed to be the first woman's
friend, or neighbor, or sister. Something.

I assumed the gothic romance belonged to a previous rider, or perhaps it was the taxi driver's. As I was
leaving the taxi, the driver yelled out the window,
"You've left your book here! You've left it in this cab!"

I read *Mistaken Intentions* and, as it turns out, the
second woman was not related to the first; they were,
at least according to the author, total strangers. And
what seemed like betrayal was, in fact, a coincidence.

Mistaken intentions are everywhere. Our director is convinced that our producer tried to catch dysentery, just to spite him. The Scottish rock star is haunted, night after night, by three men in Bangkok laughing at the fortune he has lost. Our cameraman's little sister, confused about why people might plant bombs in London, thinks that the IRA is out to get her, that they tracked her down, are trying to ruin her vacation, and want to kill her, having found out that she is, after all, one hundred percent Irish. It all reminds me of a party I went to in Westminster.

The production assistant's neighbor, boasting connections, invited us to the opening of a political advertising firm in Westminster. Fifty people were marching in front of the office building, shouting anti-apartheid slogans, banging their fists on passing cars. The production assistant's neighbor, whose connection amounted to having slept with the secretary, assured us, over the screams, that there would be cases of champagne.

The political advertising firm, it turned out, had been established to represent certain individuals in South Africa and their interests in Namibia. A man with a polka-dot tie approached us to deny the rumor that he had planned the demonstration as a publicity stunt. The secretary kept apologizing for the sudden disappearance of all the champagne. I drank Scotch and innocently spoke to guests. One of them, a man from the Foreign Office, tried to describe certain repatriation legislation pending in the House of Commons: "The idea is to pay each West Indian three thousand pounds—how shall I say?—to go from whence they came."

I tried to object during his description, but was afraid of passing out: He kept filling my glass, exposing statistics, scheduling and rescheduling a personal tour of Whitehall. Later a woman from Cape Town gave me the phone number of her hotel.

When I told Peter—the man I have to share a flat with—about the man from the Foreign Office, he wasn't surprised. He was barely interested. Peter talks about nothing but sex and money. He has stacks of imported pornography, and books with titles like *A Wine Lover's Guide to Opera* and *A Porcelain Lover's Guide to Great English Country Houses*. He lives beyond his means and needs to share his flat so he can continue buying expensive wine, going to the opera, and paying the mortgage on his country house.

I'm not sure where the porcelain fits in. I haven't seen any porcelain around the flat. Perhaps he hides it instead of the pornography.

When he is in London, which is usually one night a

week, Peter brings friends over for drinks. First they drink all the wine, then the gin, and finally the beer. The guests are always doctors, lawyers, and stockbrokers, or inheritors like Peter. At around one in the morning, when there are only inheritors, Peter tells his Princess Margaret story. A few years ago there was a luncheon given that included among its guests both Peter and Princess Margaret. To the astonishment of everyone, Peter fell sound asleep, and, according to Peter, he and Princess Margaret haven't spoken since. Each time he tells the story, the guest list becomes smaller and smaller, and his nap becomes longer and longer, until there is no one left but Princess Margaret, and Peter with his head in a salad.

After all the guests have gone, Peter puts the glasses on the mantel and calls a woman named Chloe. He gets ready to leave, and I won't see him until the next week, when he will arrive with new friends and more bottles. He always looks embarrassed when he leaves, as if he knows that I know Chloe is a prostitute.

The old questions. The old answers and the old questions are best, but people still want the most for their money.

I found my flat through an agency that specializes in "connecting flatmates of civilized backgrounds." After

I walked in, a middle-aged woman sat me in a chair and said, "You know we don't take just anybody." I smiled, trying to seem civilized. She told me about her first husband's family, once prominent in the Indian Civil Service, still remembered in Madras. I continued smiling. She told me about her own childhood in Kenya, and her difficult romance with her second husband, an army officer who spent a good deal of time away from home. When I thought about it afterward, I realized Kenya was the test.

Peter's flat was the least expensive, but the middle-aged woman insisted I first look at something respectable. She sent me to a flat in St. John's Wood owned by two middle-aged sisters. The sisters worked in the same office, slept in the same bedroom, and seemed quietly insane.

I was then sent to a flat in Fulham owned by a psychiatrist who told me about a new system he had developed for diagnosing personality disorders. "I want to pin down the problem on appearances alone," he said. "For instance, certain schizophrenics shake in certain ways. Bulimics have marks on their knuckles from sticking their fingers down their throats." He showed me a photograph of a man with blue hair and blue tattoos all over his body. "He wants to change colors, therefore, he wants to change sexes." The psychiatrist held his finger next to the man's mouth. "You can't actually tell from the photograph, but he has even had the dentist put little blue stones in all his teeth." The psychiatrist was a nervous wreck. He kept checking his wristwatch, running into the kitchen. His hands shook when he talked.

I spent an entire afternoon in Battersea at the house of impoverished German aristocrats. The mother refused to speak English, the father was dead, and the family estate was in Poland. The son, who seemed to be in his thirties, met me at the door. He told me that he wanted to be a conductor. I drank hot chocolate while he talked about great conductors, how von Karajan or Furtwängler wouldn't hesitate to slap a soloist or storm off stage during a concert. The daughter, who came home later, was a teenager who wanted to be a movie star. She had just seen *Babes on Broadway* and began translating the lyrics for her mother. "Wir verliessen Topeka, verliessen Eureka, um eine neue Karriere anzufangen." She stopped for a moment. "Oh, I've forgotten!" she said to me. "Except for the last part." She turned toward her mother. "Und wir sind Babys am Broadway jetzt!"

The old questions. In German, "*wo*" looks and sounds like "who," but actually means "where." And "*wer*" looks and sounds very much like "where," but actually means "who." With the German aristocrats, I tried using my high school German. The mother was describing a restaurant, and I asked out of curiosity, "Und wer haben Sie gegessen?" which means, of course, "Who did you eat, Frau von Heuren?"

The only cast member who has been to Dubrovnik is the actor who is actually a musician. He has a supporting role as the rock singer's best friend, and in real life he is a lutanist and an authority on Renaissance music. He explained that he was scheduled to play a cruise later in the summer, and that in the fall he was scheduled to write the music for a television biography of Rubens. He doesn't want to give up the cruise, which is going, among other places, to the Galápagos Islands. On his last cruise, in the eastern Mediterranean, he had had an affair in Tel Aviv with an Israeli soldier. "I learned how to fire a gun," he said. "It was thrilling."

He is thinking of writing the score for our film, but the story takes place in the late 1970s, and it would be his first attempt at anything contemporary.

"I distrust the new," he said. "Of course, most people feel that way now, which helps explain this place." He told me about the wave of nostalgia flooding England—people taking out their central heating, combing through deserted warehouses for authentic Victorian fabric, using Georgian recipes, rereading

Restoration comedies, listening to troubadour music, fawning over Romanesque architecture. "And they're flocking to these sorts of places, tearooms that play Gracie Fields records and put Gentleman's Relish on toast, as if it were 1937."

He finished his own toast and offered me a ride back to Belgravia.

From whence they came. Back where they came from. Homeward bound. Accounts did vary, but they concurred on one thing: The man in New Zealand didn't get a free ride. The airline refused to fly him home, and evidently he had to wait until his family and friends could get the money together for a plane ticket.

He had wanted to go to Oakland, and he ended up in debt. His instincts—to get on the plane, not to get off the plane, to leave home in the first place—had betrayed him.

"Because I love you," is an old answer. Lately, I have been calling old girlfriends long distance to suggest that they quit their jobs and immediately move to London.

They always ask why. Why should I quit my job,

which pays me twelve thousand dollars a year? Why should I leave my rent-stabilized apartment in Manhattan, which costs me eight hundred dollars a month and still has your name on the lease? Why?

I always present an economic argument—discount flights, cheap theater tickets, favorable exchange rates. It's more efficient for you to live in London. You really have no other choice.

They always say yes, yes, see you next week. And we both laugh, on our own side of the Atlantic, knowing, positively believing, that we're both kidding; knowing—instinctively—that it's all a joke.

At a party, I met a mercenary. He had fought Communists in Afghanistan before fighting Communists in Nicaragua. He described a process invented by the Russians to strip the skin off Afghan rebels. "It was psychological warfare disguised as chemical warfare," he said. "The Moslem believes in the 'pure warrior,' sanctity of the body, that sort of thing. When he saw row after row of bodies with the skin peeling off, he went mad." The mercenary drank his champagne. "A Moslem believes the skinless soul is doomed. Gone to hell."

■ ■ ■

At a restaurant in Chelsea, everything is à la carte. The waitress is Canadian and she insists that I am Canadian. She won't take no for an answer.

"Well, where are you from, then?" she says.

Los Angeles. Jamaica. Kansas. The Brown Islands.

"I just walked over from Belgravia," I tell her.

The effort made, the stamp licked, the ticket stamped, and still things end up in wrong places. A bomb in Antwerp was scheduled for a synagogue, but the terrorist's map had a misprint, and he blew up a block of jewelry stores. Diamonds filled the streets, clogged up ventilation systems, dropped out of rain gutters. In a rare moment, our producer and our director met for lunch. The film will be shot in Blackpool, the director's birthplace. Dubrovnik must be saved for later.

Everyone is relieved. The rock star is relieved, and tickets for his first stadium date go on sale next week. The production assistant is relieved that she will be home in time for the new television season. And my flatmate is relieved. He is certain that he will get twenty pounds more a week from his next American.

I tell all this to the Canadian waitress, and she says, "Where is your next movie? Where will you go then?"

And then where will you go?

And then where?

Centaurs

The smartest man in our law-school class told me he wanted to be an actor. He is short and awkward, and he has a comical problem with his *rs*. Once, he grabbed my hand and said, "Sheila, I made a terrible mistake leaving the stage." I like the idea of private failure. There must be chief executive officers harboring secret dreams of teaching high school English.

Inertia seems to be getting me through law school. I don't move much. I wait for a professor to intimidate me into the subject at hand: arson, divorce, whatever. I am particularly fascinated with the predicament of battered husbands. Not fascinated enough to do anything about it, but I don't mind reading the cases. My tax professor told me I'm not so different from my classmates. I suppose he meant the remark to be comforting.

If some man—say, X—runs a mink farm, and another, Y, is exploding dynamite next door, Y does not have to pay X in the event the mink eat their kittens from the shock of the explosion. It's the law.

I have a private life but not a personal one. Mostly, I smoke Dunhill cigarettes, put unwhipped cream on things, and reread early Evelyn Waugh novels. In private, one could argue, I'm English.

A man from Yale who wants to go into entertainment law offered to buy me dinner. We chatted about the various apartments he had had in New York, his stint in television, his midwestern roots. When we got back to his apartment and undressed, he said, "Do it to me, sweetie." Now when we see each other, which is about twelve times a day, he acts as if we were once partners in some sort of class project.

If a railroad employee, X, thinks he is tripping over a bundle of newspapers, but is in fact tripping over a can of dynamite, and the explosion causes Y to drop a valuable family heirloom, could Y sue the railroad company for the cost of her grandmother's Hummel figurine? I don't know, because I wasn't paying attention that day.

At a mandatory law-school party, a lady law professor from another university asked me to show her which were the law students and which were the dates. She just assumed I wasn't a date. After most of the guests had left, she broached the subject of alternative families. She said that lesbian motherhood was fascinating but doomed as an institution. I told her that I liked her Laura Ashley dress.

I have one friend. He is homosexual and also likes Evelyn Waugh. Sometimes he even does imitations of the characters. He calls most people philistines, and often walks into Evidence and says, "I got positively no sleep last night." I usually believe him.

At a mandatory tea at the Dean's house, I met the Dean's wife. She is an illustrator of children's books and a gourmet cook. After a few preliminary remarks, she asked if I wanted her recipe for crème brûlée. I suppose she thought I was different from the other law students.

The editor of the law review lives across the street. She used to be a nun, but now she wears hiking boots and smokes mentholated cigarettes. After she left the convent and before she entered law school, she worked at the men's cologne counter of a large department store. Sometimes she has dinner parties and drinks too much whiskey. I guess another "terrible beauty is born." But how and when? Did she just wake up one morning and head for the nearest men's cologne counter? Perhaps it happened gradually (she is about forty-five)—a rosary in one hand, a Budweiser in the other; half saint, half goat.

People in law school, like people in general, try to be pleasant, and like people in general they often fail. Law students, I have noticed, tend to eat three-quarters of a sandwich and then wrap the remainder in foil, right there out in the open. One law student who is handicapped asks people to buy him hot chocolate around lunchtime because his wheelchair can't get near the vending machines. The other law students, busy wrapping, usually don't hear him.

My Jurisprudence professor decided to hold class in his apartment so it could turn into a party. He had a copy of *Soviet Life* in the bathroom and talked about how much money he would be making if he weren't a law professor. He lives with one of his former students. She is a judge and wears the same clothes as he does: boots, blue jeans, blazers. They are both, as fate would have it, from the same Chicago suburb. She came up to me with a plateful of cucumbers and smiled. I wanted to tell her that while insanity may be a defense for homicide, it is not a defense for a plateful of cucumbers; she always has a ravaged, insane look on her face.

As a child I wanted to be an actress. More recently

I have toyed with the idea of becoming a chief executive officer.

Each year, we eagerly await the Malpractice party and the White-Collar Crime party. The Malpractice party comes in October and is made up of law students and medical students. The White-Collar Crime party comes in February and is made up of law students and business students. One wonders: Left to their own devices, do the medical students and business students also meet? Is there such an animal as the Hospital Administrator's party?

Soon we will be reading about a woman who signed up in advance for thirty thousand dollars' worth of dance lessons. I am not sure if she was hit by a car on the way to her first lesson and wanted all her money back, or if she never learned to dance and blew up the studio with dynamite. Perhaps she was black, or a man, or handicapped, and they gave her inferior lessons. I just don't know.

In law school, you can feel boredom go from the benign to the malignant. You can see people with quarters of tuna-salad sandwiches in their briefcases arguing about mink farms. You could, with a little patience and finesse, get yourself invited to a party, where the food and the liquor are usually free.

Law students, unlike other students, tend to have umbrellas. I feel even more English when it rains and find myself saying things like "Excuse me, I have to go to the loo."

Some of the more interesting stereotyped characteristics of law students: unshaven, impotent, dirty, overweight, devout, narrow-minded, humorless. Or if they're women: frigid, tall, overweight, giddy. If you have ever seen a law-school catalogue, you know there are very few pictures.

I could be wrong, of course. Perhaps the man from Yale said, "Do it to me, mama," not "sweetie." This would make more sense, since I am taller than he is. But if I had to go through it all over again and he did say "sweetie," I would tell him never under any circumstances to use both an imperative and a diminutive in the same sentence—especially in bed.

The other day, I was on my way to class when the man from Yale come out of nowhere and said to me, "Where are you galloping off to?"

At law-school parties, men and women talk to each other as if there were no difference between men and women. The law students and the dates act as if there were no difference between the law students and the dates. Of course, the dates don't understand all this talk about law, unless they happen to be judges. Sometimes the women talk about feminism, and sometimes the men talk about sports, but we eventually leave those topics to the extremists and drift off onto less sacred subjects. I have never heard Evelyn Waugh's name brought up at a law-school party, not even at the ex-nun's house. My homosexual friend has better things to do, and I usually don't open my mouth, even though I am a baseball fan.

Transformations, sublimations, things becoming other things. Yesterday, I had a Reuben potato— certainly the centaur of modern delicatessen food. As I prodded the melted cheese from some trace of Russian dressing, I tried to recall if any law-school parties so far have been catered. I am becoming a lawyer.

The Most Important Thing

I take photographs, although I rarely photograph people. People—to me, at least—don't have features, they have profiles and presences, shapes and space; I photograph objects of my own construction. Perhaps it's possible to find faces in my photographs, or bodies, or parts of bodies, but I see only bent wire and shadow. To support myself, I work as a supervisor for the city's public-assistance commission. Most of the other supervisors have German-sounding names, and the secretaries have Polish, or Czech, or vaguely Eastern European names; I am Jewish, with a Jewish name, and, because there are so few Jews in this city,

I often feel Jewish—at work, for example—by contrast. Sometimes I think of myself as a bureaucrat. Once a week, in the lobby of what used to be the county courthouse, I oversee the distribution of welfare checks to people without permanent addresses. The people coming to pick up their checks are usually black and often women; the clerks who actually hand out the checks are black women; I sit behind the clerks and, except for the police, am the white man. Photographer; Jew; bureaucrat. I am certainly more than these things, and, I suppose, incompletely each of them, but recently, while eating dinner with a woman I had never met before, they seemed to have nothing to do with me.

Her husband is a man I work with, another supervisor on the public-assistance commission, named Berger. He and I became friendly after he found out about my photographs, and over lunch, and then in bars after work, he would talk, contradictorily, it seemed, about his interest in woodworking: He made sculptures out of wood, he only made furniture; he was going to a "woodworking camp" in the summer, he had been to the camp in previous summers and was never going back. Or about his wife: She had lived in Spain, she had lived in Africa; she was going back to school, she had already gone back to school; she worked as a translator, or as an engineer, or she spent her days shopping for food. He never asked about my photographs, or if I had a wife, which I haven't, but I enjoyed listening to Berger because he seemed to make up his stories as he went along. He did not seem serious about woodworking and spoke indifferently about his wife. Eventually he invited me over for dinner to see his wood pieces and to meet his wife, and I half-expected to find an empty house with a single narrow mattress on the floor.

Berger was waiting at the end of his driveway when I arrived. He led me into his house, then through its cluttered rooms, pointing out half-completed tables and chairs, half-stained bookcases, "sculptures." There were unopened cans of stain everywhere, and spray cans of varnish, hand tools on the unfinished tables, a saw on the back porch, and another in the kitchen; laundry baskets filled with folded towels or women's underwear, or overturned laundry baskets. He pointed briefly at a room with a half-closed door and said that his wife was teaching Spanish to a couple planning a trip to Spain, then he led me into a bathroom, where he was cooking something in an electric frying pan. He was in the middle of remodeling his kitchen, he explained, and he and his wife cooked in the bathroom. There was a dish drainer in the bathtub, and bowls of cut-up vegetables on the floor, hand tools and cooking utensils on top of the toilet, spices in the medicine chest. We drank beer while he cooked. He didn't seem to want to talk about woodworking or his wife (I could hear her Spanish underneath Berger's cooking noises), and I talked about myself, or rather, about my photography. I had just read a magazine article about a kind of topologist called a knot theorist. The knot theorist had revolutionary ideas about knots in the fourth dimension and, in trying to imagine what a fourth dimension looked like, he had cast the shadows of knots on a screen, which reminded me of what I was doing with wire. "Topology," I began, "is a kind of geometry." Berger's wife suddenly appeared in the bathroom doorway. "They're not staying," she said, and walked out.

Then there was confusion. The couple, who were standing behind Berger's wife, tried to chat in Spanish with Berger. "Have a seat," Berger said to me, and he disappeared with the couple: his wife, too, seemed to have disappeared. I took another beer from the cooler on the bathroom floor and went to sit down at the dining-room table. Berger soon returned without the couple and began to carry bowls of food back and forth between the dining room and the bathroom. "So," he said, sitting down between trips. "Geometry." His wife reappeared and sat down quietly. "Oh, this is my wife," he said before running out again. "We're listening," he shouted from the bathroom.

"Topology," I said, "is the study of shapes and space." I began to explain to her, shouting occasionally in the direction of the bathroom, how the magazine article had influenced me. Before, I explained, I had photographed the shadows of bent wire, and now I wanted to tie the wire in knots before creating a shadow. "I don't know anything about photography," she said. "Except when to press the button."

Berger returned to the table, and he and his wife discussed the food. He had cooked certain Spanish dishes, and she told him how much the meat and vegetables would have cost in Spain, and estimated how much money they could have saved if she had shipped home more olive oil during her last visit. I asked her if she missed Spain. "Only the prices," she said.

Her face was heavy and pale, with a faint mustache; she kept her black hair behind her ears with black plastic clips; her hands were small and soiled, and she had bitten off her fingernails. And yet her tiny eyes were powerful, and she had an assured voice: She had the manner, really, of a vain woman, or of a more feminine woman.

Berger and I began to talk about work while his wife ate very quickly. "It was better the last time you made it," she said, interrupting me and pointing at a bowl on Berger's side of the table. I wanted to include her in the conversation. I told her how all the supervisors on the public-assistance commission had German-sounding names, and the secretaries had Eastern European names; it was like a fantasy, I explained, like turn-of-the-century Prague, or some other place in Eastern Europe if the Germans had won the war. "And I have a Jewish name," I said, with a laugh. "Oh, I don't think people hold that against each other anymore," she said.

Berger continued to talk about work. He asked me if I preferred the commission's new offices in the municipal courthouse to its old offices in the county courthouse. (Berger began working for the public-assistance commission a month after the move.) "The *county* courthouse?" said Berger's wife. "Now what's that?"

I explained to her that the county had been turning over control of various services and buildings to its municipalities; the county courthouse's lobby was now used to distribute the city's welfare checks and its basement was the city's free testing site for venereal diseases. "The people wanting to get tested are encouraged to use pseudonyms," I said. "A mayoral directive entitles them to free parking, and they identify themselves to the parking-lot attendants by saying, 'I am here to see Mary.' Sometimes, apparently, some of them assume that the people waiting in line to pick up their welfare checks are waiting to get tested for venereal diseases, and they also wait, until they reach one of the secretaries and say, 'My name is John and I am here to see Mary.' " Berger's wife refilled her plate. "I can't stand waiting," she said.

We finished eating, and Berger brought out a box of photographs. Before he had met his wife, he explained, he had worked as a fisherman off Cape Cod, and his wife had worked as an engineer all over Africa. There were pictures of Berger on a fishing boat and pictures of his wife in Africa. She smiled broadly at one of the pictures and told a story about waiting for a bus somewhere in Ghana.

She wanted to go to the next village, she said, which was a day's journey away by bus, but the bus only stopped at the village on the first day of the month. The first month she waited all day, but the bus never came. The next month she overslept and missed the bus. The third month she began to wait at sunrise, and by noon there were dozens of other people from nearby villages also waiting. She and two Norwegian men were the only white people. In West Africa, she knew, custom demanded that whites board the bus before anyone else and sit in the front rows but, when the bus arrived, she boarded last and stood in the back with the old black women. A few miles out of the village there was a military checkpoint, and the first three rows of passengers—including the Norwegians, who were sitting just behind the driver—were taken off the bus and never heard from again. "If I had sat where I could have," she said, "I would probably have been shot."

A story's ability to suggest something—its moral— is, I once read, the privilege of its teller. Take the knot theorist: A regular knot, he told his interviewer, in spite of its twistings and turnings, is always an un- broken strand; a knot in the fourth dimension— twistings and turnings, moving unbroken through time—has an unknowable shape, but one that might be thought of as the shape of a person's life. The moral of the knot theorist's remarks, I imagined, was that something, in everyone's life, doesn't change. Berg- er's wife's story about Africa, however, had no moral. She didn't mean to suggest anything: The story stopped with her.

"Well," she said suddenly. "There aren't any more pictures of me, so I'm going to bed."

I have made no impression on you, I thought. Ev- erything starts and stops with you, and I am just a man who isn't your husband. "Goodnight," I said.

The viewer's privilege is to disbelieve the camera, to think that something in the photograph (and usu- ally, therefore, the most important thing) is missing. Berger's wife said goodnight to me and then to Berger with the same voice, the same nod. At no time during the evening did anything resembling love pass between them.

After his wife left, Berger talked late into the night about being a fisherman; his eyes hovered and leapt as he spoke. He told me that he loved the open sea, what he called "the wholeness of it," the way the sky and the water become one. There was something feminine, I thought, in his love of the ocean, not a theorizing, and not a fearlessness, but a suspicion, a secret smile. I have lived in this place all my life, far from any ocean. Does Berger know something I will never know?

When the time came to leave, Berger walked me outside. I had parked my car at the end of his driveway, behind his house and past the reach of the streetlights. He left me alone in the dark driveway, and I tried to remember my arrival, if, perhaps, there was something to avoid: scattered tools, flower pots, garbage cans, bicycles, or just the darkened edges of the house itself. I avoided them all, and carelessly, as if they weren't there, as if—and thinking it struck me as a man's privilege, or a photographer's conceit— they never would be there. Then the driveway turned into the road. Empty white expanse.

Wartime

Ealing is a suburb west of London that used to be famous for its movie studios. Now the movie studios make television shows, and most people here are waiting around for the Indians to take over. The woman I am staying with lives in a new house near Ealing Broadway. She is registered for two boarders, but often fits up to ten. Mrs. Concannon lives in fear that the neighbors want to report this to the police. "They're just jealous of me because I can afford a microwave and nice things," she says. "And they're jealous of my daughter Mary's good looks." Mary is twenty, and has long, red hair that she perms herself.

I don't know what to call Mrs. Concannon. Sometimes I say "Mrs. Concannon," which is her ex-husband's name. (Her husband ran off with a Polish waitress when they lived in Chicago.) But then she says, "That's my man's name, and he's long gone. Try Murphy. It's good enough for my brothers." So I call her Mrs. Murphy. "Stop it, honeychild," she'll say. "Call me Eileen." When I finally called her Eileen, she said, "Mrs. Concannon to you, mister." If I have any questions, I ask Mary.

Mary wants to be a fashion designer. She spends all day making large model twills out of construction paper. When one of the Italian boys walks through the kitchen in a towel, Mary says, "He'll do." Mary doesn't talk to me. She knows I am waiting for the shampoo heiress.

For years, perhaps since I was fourteen, I have loved a shampoo heiress. I call Susan "the shampoo heiress" because her father owns a large cosmetics factory. I write her long, witty letters; I use her company's shampoo. She is very beautiful, I think, except for a slightly discolored front tooth. Sometimes I tell her to get the tooth capped. She says it's too expensive. Is she kidding me?

I have followed Susan all over the United States, and I have followed her to Europe. She teaches the fifth grade at a school in Des Moines, but always leaves

the Middle West during vacations. Last month she
called and told me to meet her in Ealing. "A week in
London, then two weeks in Paris," she said. I have a
three-week vacation every June.

On my last trip to Europe—my only trip, in fact—
Susan and I went to Italy. Sometimes, while I'm sitting in Mrs. Concannon's backyard, I think of us
together in Florence: Susan, in her yellow sundress,
my hand on her damp back. We stayed in a little hotel
where the bed was too short for both of us.

When I arrived at Mrs. Concannon's, there was a
telegram from Susan's stepmother saying that Susan
had to go to Mallorca and would be two weeks late.
Susan lived with Mrs. Concannon while she went to
college in London, so I am staying as a special guest in
the front room. Mrs. Concannon has a kind of lava
lamp attached to the fireplace. She showed me how it
works, then she told me never to turn it on again
because it uses up too much electricity.

I have come in the midst of turmoil: There are
threats of a major newspaper war. While other places
in similar states of decay worry about postal strikes, or
rail strikes, or terrorists, here everyone quivers at the
prospect of a newspaper war. The last one was over
bingo; the next one is supposed to be about rock gossip. Already, Mary is talking about which singer of
which group often hits his mother or doesn't care for

Chinese food. She buys five papers a day to keep up with her friends. The only thing I've read since I've been here is the Ealing *Leader*. Yesterday, a story on the front page read: "A matchstick violin made by a prisoner serving life for murder has been sold for £170 at Sotheby's." Mrs. Concannon was more interested in the announcement of a concert planned for the fall. She showed the article to me at lunch: "An open-air rock festival has prompted fears of an invasion by drug addicts."

Mrs. Concannon blames the concert on the Indians. Mary tried to convince her mother that the group in question was quite clean-cut by describing all the members' wives and children. Mrs. Concannon said, "Send them back to Bombay." She was probably thinking of the Indian couple down the block. They run a boardinghouse and evidently get ten pounds more a week than Mrs. Concannon for each of their boarders. Mrs. Concannon says the Ramandandis are registered for two boarders but have kept five American girls since early February. She often threatens to call the police.

Sometimes Mrs. Concannon's son, Patrick, stops by. Patrick is thirty-three and always asks me about Arlo Guthrie. One night Patrick told me about himself: "I was a mod, you see. I couldn't have been a hippie. They was mostly middle-class kids who didn't have to get up for work the next day. I always said the women were attractive, though, the women with their hair down. But they wouldn't go for me. If you're a hippie, you don't go for mods, now, do you?"

Patrick asked if I wanted to drive with him to Hammersmith and hear country-western music, but I said no. Instead, I watched Mary make a paper patch of Donegal tweed. It was the last in a series of tweeds she had been working on for nine months, and, as she put the unused scraps of paper into the garbage, I felt as if I were witnessing part of her life ending. Just before she left the room, Mary said, "The herringbone patch is probably the best in my year, but I still think it's awful." She showed me the patch and went to bed.

Mrs. Concannon is from Ireland. She married Padraic Concannon and moved to America, gave birth to six children, and came to London after her husband left her. Susan idolizes Mrs. Concannon. When I arrived at her house, Mrs. Concannon hugged me and said, "You're our Susan's friend who used to call all the time. In all my years with the students, I loved Susan best. She always brought me avocado pears and always looked so pretty. Oh, she is a darling girl." Mrs. Concannon has the strangest accent I have ever heard—a sort of Irish-Southern combination. She must have lived in a black neighborhood in Chicago.

One night last week, I was alone with Sabine, the

French student from Toulouse. She wanted to apply for a job as a stewardess, and I offered to help her with the letter. She was using a brown felt-tip pen on brown stationery. I suggested she type the letter; I offered to help her find a typewriter. "I have a good face," she said. "That's enough. A good face and a good letter is too good. People don't like that." Her American boyfriend picked her up at ten, and I haven't seen her since.

People seem to be disappearing around here. All the students are traveling, or in London, or out. Tonight, there are only Mrs. Concannon and myself. She reaches behind the turpentine for her Irish whiskey and makes us both some "punch." She tells me her husband will come back when he hears how rich she is, and she shows me her Barclay's book. "Two thousand pounds, mister. You can't laugh at that." She tells me Irish jokes. "St. Patrick drove the snakes out of Ireland, and you know what happened? They're all cops in New York." She helps me pack my suitcases. I am flying home tomorrow.

I don't tell Mrs. Concannon, but I am relieved that Susan never showed up. Mrs. Concannon says, "A mighty shame, that," sounding English at last. "You've waited so very long."

In the spring, I saw Susan at her brother's apartment in Manhattan. Her brother is a film historian, and we waited all night for a party of his to end so we could watch old movies on his VCR. Most of the other people at the party were also film historians, and I accidentally sat in on a conversation about narrative structure. Two men and a woman, each fluent in the dreams of another generation, were lamenting the lack of dénouement in thirties musicals, artificial endings, things just stopping. Susan said she wanted to be alone with her brother. We could meet the next day, she told me. In the morning she phoned from the airport to say goodbye.

I watch Mrs. Concannon make the tea, and I want to tell her that I understand why she waits. She is waiting for the police, for the drug addicts, for her husband, all promising to bring her their peculiar brands of finality. She knows they will never come; she knows she is imagining them. She knows what I know—none of us want peace.

Home

I knew a lot of Europeans in New York. Many of them snorted heroin. Some snorted heroin and cocaine at the same time. Many worked or wanted to work in the fashion industry; the others, it was generally assumed, were diplomats. Nearly all the European women who weren't diplomats married homosexual men to get their green cards. European men, an American woman told me, maintain affairs back home.

In New York, I knew a Swiss art critic on graduate fellowship in physics who looked insulted if no one asked to hear his Romansh. I ate dinner at a Burmese restaurant, a Nepalese restaurant, a Venezuelan restaurant. I met a model who was half-Spanish, half-Vietnamese.

I worked as a secretary for a film director, who, because I was a man, refused to learn my first name. He had two agents, a corporate law firm, and several accountants. He had one wife, two ex-wives, seven children, a housekeeper, a cleaning lady, and a cook. When he moved into his new apartment, I was the one who scrubbed the movers' marks off the floors. He was imprecise about his childhood. Sometimes he grew up in Berlin, sometimes Warsaw. He knew nothing about me. I knew how much money he made because my primary duty was going through garbage to find financial statements and stock certificates he had thrown away by mistake.

In New York, in line at a bank, I stood behind a woman with seven hundred thousand dollars in her checking account.

I invited an old friend over to my new apartment. We had a glass of wine. We smoked a joint. I had to call the paramedics because she thought her heart might stop. While one of the paramedics administered oxygen, and the other wrote up the report, the policeman who had accompanied them said to me, "This always happens to my wife when she gets bad weed."

Before I found my apartment, I stayed in a neighborhood where the only white people were me, the people I was staying with, and the concentration-camp survivor who ran the laundromat. One night, the girl whose parents had paid the apartment's five-thousand-dollar deposit came through the door crying. She had been mugged, she said, at knife point, by two ten-year-olds, who, after taking her purse, reached up and slapped her face. At the police station, she identified the two boys in a line-up; they turned out to be thirteen and fourteen, and suspects in a throat slashing.

My first apartment in New York had a courtyard. The friend who helped me move stuck his head out the window, into the courtyard. "The only noise you'll hear," he said, "is white noise. Air-conditioners. Classical music." Later that night, we both looked out the window at the two women screaming in the apartment across the courtyard. "Your mother was a whore," one said to the other, which was all we could make out until the silence, and then the thud as the woman who had just been hit landed on the floor.

I spent my days in the personal assistants' circuit. Film publicists' assistants, Broadway producers' interns, agents' girl fridays, periodontists' receptionists, the film director's accountants' Pakistani bookkeeper. Some, like me, had just begun; most had been there for years. Some had special Dictaphone equipment and specially ordered chairs, some waited hours in copy shops. Some lied, some stole, some were loyal and without ambition. Every one was different— except for the thing they had in common, which was hate.

I talked to famous people on the telephone: I talked to society hostesses, a major-league-baseball manager, actors with papal-like privileges. I talked to immigrants wanting checkups because the Immigration Service had confused the film director's office phone number with the number of a free clinic. I talked to the man from Queens who usually called pretending to be a famous film director. "I'm the greatest," he would say. "Better than Cecil B. De Miller."

I spent less and less time with people I had known before and more time alone or at parties. I went to parties diligently, with high spirits, the way many people read the newspaper. I went for covert reasons— for sex, I suppose. I went for no reason. When I went to find a change and soon found more of the same, I left or stayed on cynically. If I met people, I met them on my way out.

A man I met at a party was a stockbroker. He took limousines everywhere. One night he picked me up in the limousine and we went to Harlem. While I stayed in the car, and he bought drugs in a deserted building, a woman wheeled a stereo system in front of the headlights. She banged on the windshield. The chauffeur got out of the car, gave her three one-hundred-dollar bills; they talked for a moment. He began to shout, into the car, at me. "Do you want to help us?" He was rubbing his palms into the cabinet corners. "We have to unscrew the legs."

I knew a woman who relocated each New York moment back to a suburban high school: Her boss, she would say, was acting like the Honor Society treasurer who wanted to be president; the waiter looked like an earth-science teacher; backstage at the ballet, she told the Russian choreographer that his pas de deux reminded her of a Sadie Hawkins dance. Meanwhile, the film director had found himself living in the next decade. He stood in his new apartment, examining his peculiar light switches, his rounded doors, his uncomfortable telephones. "In ten years everyone will have these," he said, possibly to his cook, who lived there, as she tried to find the handles on his new kitchen cupboards.

A man I met had gone to Harvard. During his junior year he wrote a poem—a sestina—in which one of the repeating phrases ended with "Says Tina." Anyone who had gone to Harvard, then or shortly thereafter, knew of this man and his sestina. He graduated and moved to New York, where I met him, and where he seemed to be in retirement.

The smartest man anyone seemed to know in New York was the philosophy instructor who lived, in a loft on West Twenty-third Street, with his much younger deaf-mute girlfriend and a dyslexic actress. The actress served as a kind of maid, in spite of her recurring cameo on a network soap opera.

I went to a party, with the philosophy instructor and the man in retirement, and met famous young writers. One talked about his hate mail. One asked another if "I would gladly pay you Tuesday for a hamburger today" was from *The Waste Land* or *The Four Quartets*. One described a certain copyright agreement which meant that, technically, she and Geoffrey Chaucer had the same literary agent.

In New York I dated a thirty-two-year-old woman and a nineteen-year-old girl. The woman used to say the most important thing in her life was kindness; she wanted to be kind, which meant, in practice, that she only read books, or saw plays and movies, that in some way involved people she had known at Yale. Her parents supported her and she would tell me, interrupting what seemed like intimate moments, how much they had paid for things in her apartment. Next to her bed there was a television set the size of a human face, which she could operate, like an adding machine, without looking. The nineteen-year-old was a second-generation hippie from Oregon who wanted to be a poet or a photographer. Eventually she dropped out of NYU to work as a secretary for a photographer's agent. While she was seeing me, she was also seeing a forty-five-year-old theater critic. She would say things like "I never read the *Times*. I read *Newsday*. *Newsday* rocks."

While the film director redubbed his movie for European release, I spent twelve-hour days with a team of sound technicians. They kept track of ironic obituaries in *Variety:* The production assistant on *You Asked for It!* who committed suicide; the opera singer who had a stroke while singing a spiritual; the starlet who slit her wrists, but on a bluff somewhere, and died of exposure. They were maniacal about crossword puzzles. They built anagrams and palindromes on the sound studio's computer system.

I thought, more than once, that people in New York shouldn't have personal lives. No affairs, no kinds of pleasure, nothing.

I lived through strikes: a garbage strike, a baseball strike, a directors' strike. I lived through two memorable snowstorms and a hurricane—or rather the promise of a hurricane; it poised itself late one evening in New York Harbor, and the next day not even the weathermen could find it.

The film director gave me a raise, and I began to go

to concerts. In the larger concert halls, there were often famous people in the audiences and usually some kind of direct or indirect violence. Smoke bombs rolled down aisles, or there were bomb threats; disputes broke out between friends over who should sit where; ushers at the opera strapped in standing-room listeners so they couldn't run for orchestra seats as the lights went down.

The apartment with the courtyard, which I learned about through an ad in the newspaper, was on the Lower East Side. There were four bedrooms and people came and went, except for the tall nervous woman who was French and lived in the front room. She drank vodka from glasses her parents sent specially for the purpose. She chain-smoked. She smelled of coffee, alcohol, cigarettes, perfume. She would come home at six o'clock in the morning and stand in the kitchen, which was next to my room, raving and sobbing. Then she would watch two hours of morning news before going to work: "For my English," she would say in her perfect English. I am not certain she slept. Her hair, which was black and splayed, was like the hair of a madwoman.

Another woman I knew was neurotic, but she wanted to get away. She lived above a wholesale fish market, across the street from the Port Authority. She asked her old boyfriend, who wanted to marry her, to take care of her thirty-five-pound cat while she went to Ireland. There were days when he forgot, or didn't have subway fare, or just didn't show up, and the cat, without food and water for some time, ate sofa stuffing and developed a bladder infection. She returned from Ireland, to the fish, to the bus fumes, to a sick cat and a floor covered with foam rubber and bloody cat urine, and began calling up friends to try to sublet her apartment. Eventually she called me, ready to take a loss, which is why I live where I do now.

I saw a woman fall perfectly on one side. She stood up. We thought she was fine. It was the middle of winter, near a subway stop. As she turned around we saw that half her coat, half her face, her purse, one hand, were immaculately covered with brown water. A young man took out a tissue and tried to clean her off. He rubbed the dirt deeper into the nape of her coat, and into the creases of her skin. "How do I look?" she asked. "Better," said the man.

I used to work for a film director. Now I work at a studio. I used to live with strangers on the Lower East Side. Now I live here, in Midtown, alone. I seem to be moving forward, or up.

One of the people who works at the studio is an accountant who has me take care of his dog on the weekends. He is, almost exactly, a prig. No liquor, no television set, no concessions. Except the telephone. He lives by himself, except for the dog, and keeps pornography hidden under his bed in a Mark Cross suitcase—from me, I suppose. His father is a banker and his mother is a sex therapist. He always talks about his parents delicately, as if they were in the next room. He is independently wealthy, uncasual, certainly a hypocrite. Often he seems to belong to a different century, to the nineteenth, or the twenty-first.

There is something feudal about the film director, and post-apocalyptic about the philosophy instructor. The man in retirement has just entered his middle twenties. Nearly everyone is some time else.

My new neighborhood has the bus station and is on the edge of the theater district, which seems to explain the street people and the AIDS victims. Like my old neighborhood, this one has a street person with his own pack of dogs, but the first time I saw the man covered with plastic bags I thought he was a garbage pile. He stood up, growled, shook off what I had just thrown on him. Of course I can't be sure about the AIDS victims, but after I saw one, I thought I always saw them.

There is a difference between the presence of pleasure and the absence of pain; between flourishing and surviving; between there and then, and here

and now. I have wondered, lately, about kinds of differences.

I went to visit my parents with virtually no luggage.
I wanted to wear sweaters from college, athletic socks
from high school—I wanted to walk around in that
kind of drag. On the plane I read in the Science section of the *Times* about life in the approaching millen-
nium: People—because of a war, or because they're
bored—will be moving out to sea, to what sounded
like renovated oil rigs, or to space stations, to the
moon. I got off the plane and my father, my mother,
my aunt, my sister, and my sister's fiancé were waiting
in the terminal. The car ride to my parents' house was
crowded, but in the back seat, with one leg touching
my sister and one leg touching her fiancé, I felt small
enough to let their legs touch each other, barely there
at all. As the car stopped in the driveway, one of them
asked if I was glad to be home. "Sure," I said, although this wasn't my home, because New York is.

I keep moving forward and up—on the subways, in
the streets, in the elevators; the studio has moved my
alcove to the top floor of its office building. But during
the day I move nowhere at all. I read scripts. I eat
lunch at my desk. Late in the afternoons my legs begin to wither, and I feel strapped-in, that I am falling
back.

I have wondered at the difference between explorers and prisoners. The explorer—in space, in time—is everywhere and always. The prisoner—if he is forgotten as he usually is—is nowhere, never. Explorers and prisoners couldn't be more different—except that they're the same. Not at home.

Under Water

In London, I live in the American ghetto. Around
Baker Street, you can see us on the weekends in our
college sweatshirts. Most of us work in banks. It's
anybody's guess what the other ones do. We all seem
to have the same names: Tom, Fred, Bill. My apartment building is right above the Baker Street station,
and on my floor there are four Toms, two Freds, and
two Bills, all American, spread out evenly among the
"luxury flats." There is also an Austrian man named
Mr. Rosenzweig, who has been living in the same
apartment for fifty years. He never opens the door
when someone knocks. The Americans always knock.

We ask for help in understanding our Electricity
Board notices, or in finding an address, or if we want
to know what "Oxon." means. Unless one of us goes
downstairs and asks the porter, we usually wind up at
Nigel's, at the end of the hall. There aren't any women
on our floor.

The bank I work for is controlled by faceless Saudi
Arabians. I was recruited out of business school for a
two-year training program. The bank found my apartment, sends me to a Tunisian beach whenever I look
exhausted, and refuses to tell me where it will send
me at the end of the two years. My roommates, Bill
and Fred, are envious when I go to Tunisia. They
work for an American bank.

I know a woman in London named Francine. She is
from Pennsylvania and came here to ghostwrite a book
on refinishing furniture. Every day she tape-records
conversations with an antique dealer. The antique
dealer, a twice-divorced millionairess from Delaware,
has a huge advance for the book, which Francine de-
scribes as "part autobiography, part feminist guide to
refinishing furniture." The millionairess doesn't know
it, but Francine actually spends most of her time writing a screenplay.

I don't know what to make of Francine. She is always alluding to these men she knows—old boy-
friends, or men she has met at the theater. I met her

for the first time at a newsagent's on Marylebone Road. We both wanted the last copy of the *International Herald Tribune,* and the Bangladeshi owner gave it to Francine ("Because I have blond hair," she later told me). We started down the street together, and I asked her out for lunch. At first I thought we might start something, but she didn't seem very interested. Now the only thing we do together is eat at expensive Indian restaurants. Francine always says that London has better Indian food than India. I guess in Francine's mind the American man—unlike Indian food—is best in his native land.

Francine lives in a house across the street from Kew Gardens, and the man living above her breeds guinea pigs. She is working on a screenplay about a writer from Pennsylvania who comes to London and lives on top of a couple who breed guinea pigs. When Francine isn't talking about where she lives, she talks about her screenplay.

The only friend of Francine's that I have actually met is another American writer, named Leonard. His plays have been put on somewhere, but Francine calls him "undeservedly successful." One night we all met for dinner. He insisted on tasting everyone else's food and talking about his new play. "It's called *Venice Ignored,*" he said, "and it's all about an American *artiste* type who goes to Venice and takes up with this

family from Arkansas." He told us that he got the idea
the month before, after meeting a family from Little
Rock in a Venetian church. "I mean, there they were,
right, with all this video equipment and their sensible
shoes. Of course I adopted them and immediately
took them everywhere. I have a picture of us all pos-
ing next to the grave of Peggy Guggenheim's dogs. I
want to blow it up and use it as a backdrop for my
play."

After Francine went to the bathroom, Leonard
said, "Poor Francine. She's just a failed writer and a
repressed lesbian. I guess that's why whenever we're
together I so enjoy talking about my writing and her
sex life." When Francine came back, Leonard made
us discuss English women. "Look around you," he
said. "Look at them. Chickens and horses, chickens
and horses. Don't you think so, Francine? Don't you
think English women can turn any place into a
barn?"

Afterward, as we waited for a train underneath
Leicester Square, Leonard led us to the edge of the
platform and pointed at rats running back and forth
across the tracks. "Vintage Eliot," he said.

Strange things sometimes happen. On my way to
work one morning, the train stopped at Oxford Cir-
cus, and we all had to get off: Someone, on the tracks
near Holborn, had discovered an unexploded bomb

from the Second World War. The crowds began to head for a different line or the telephones, and a woman with light hair and a small, black briefcase asked me for change. She opened the case to get out a pound note and all her things fell onto the floor: a set of socket wrenches, money, paint tubes, small photographs of herself in various costumes. She let out a little scream, and I helped her pick up the things. She thanked me, asked me to forget about the change, and walked away.

I decided to follow her, waiting a moment before following her up the escalator. When I reached the top, I saw her standing near the telephones opening up her briefcase. Again everything emptied onto the floor. She seemed surprised, as if it hadn't just happened. I came up to her and smiled. Not saying anything, I bent down and began to put the wrenches back into the case. A moment before, while she was asking for change, she had struck me as aloof, as if it were her birthright to get change from Americans, or let them help her if something went wrong. But she was different now. She started telling me about herself. She said she was a window dresser—or "display designer," as she called it—and she was already an hour late for work. She told me she had overslept because her roommate had moved out, and she was supposed to be at work that morning by seven-thirty.

Her store was changing its displays. "We're doing this brilliant Guatemalan scheme," she said. She showed me a picture of herself in what I presumed to be Guatemalan clothes. Her name was Sarah Heseltine, and she lived in Islington. "It's very trendy," she said, "but I like it anyway."

She invited me over for dinner the next night, and, when I arrived, there wasn't any place for us to sit down. "My old flatmate finished moving out yesterday," she said. She told me that he had taken all the furniture and most of the dishes. "He's left me some forks and a corkscrew." We sat on the floor and drank the wine I had brought.

"It wasn't as if I fancied him, or anything like that," she said. "But he did help me quite a bit with my work. I would dress up, using all the different schemes the store was thinking about for the coming month. I'd shop around for the right clothes and things, to establish the mood. Then Henry, my flatmate, would take pictures of each one. The store manager would choose the scheme that looked best. It's rather a powerful position, really—mine, I mean. If I was dead set against a certain scheme, I would intentionally look awful in the pictures. The store manager had this Nigerian scheme that I absolutely hated. So I just wrapped the turbans all wrong and actually ruined the makeup. And with a little help from Henry—you know, bad lighting, that sort of thing—I managed to nip it in the bud."

I asked her what she was going to do now, who was going to take pictures of her.

"I suppose Henry will," she said. "He's only moved across the road."

After the wine was gone, she told me that she was twenty-three, and that her ambition was to design window displays for the Liberty department store. "They pay more than Harrods," she explained. I told her how old I was, and she said that she had thought I was much older because I was losing my hair.

The following weekend was long because of a bank holiday, and Bill and Fred talked about going to Amsterdam, but Fred got bronchitis, and Bill wasn't about to go alone. Then it was Monday, and the weekend was over. I was getting ready to go to Sarah's. She was having a party, and I told her that I might stop by around nine. I was sure I would be the only American, and I thought about trying to appear more English. I remembered Francine's telling me that the only difference between English and American men is facial expressions—she thinks the English don't have any. I stood in front of the mirror, pretending to wonder what I would look like without facial expressions.

On my way out, I ran into Bill. He had just finished playing in a baseball game. They have these pickup teams and they always play until it gets dark. I noticed that he was wearing my T-shirt. He must have run home to beat the rain, because he was all out of breath. We spoke to each other, and then he got into the elevator.

The rain had stopped, but the sidewalks and the cars were still wet. The evening felt damp, as usual, and the sky was a sick, gray color. That afternoon, I had taken a walk in Regent's Park. It was late May, and the tulips had died. The one time I talked to Mr. Rosenzweig he talked about flowers. He recited a schedule for the blooming of daffodils, tulips, wisteria, rhododendrons, and roses. "When the roses bloom," he said, "then you must go to Walpole Park." I tried to remember that night when the roses were supposed to bloom.

There is something numbing about London at night. It's always too quiet, as if the noises of the next day will never come.

I took the train to Sarah's and got off at the Angel tube station. The streets were narrow and twisted, and I kept getting lost. (Even now, I still get lost.) I was not actually invited to the party, but I asked Sarah if I could come anyway. As I walked around the canal, I wasn't sure why I wanted to go.

I have been spending a lot of time in Islington since I met Sarah, and once, in one of those narrow streets,

I ran into Francine's friend Leonard. He told me he also lived in Islington, although that first time I met him he told me he lived in Hampstead. He wanted to know if I had spoken to Francine, whether I had heard about her latest obsession. I said no, and he told me about some young writer back home who had just become famous. "Here we have the case of a man—or boy, rather—who is a homosexual accountant, and his father has a brain tumor. So he writes this novel all about a homosexual accountant whose father has a brain tumor. Critics love it. Homosexuals love it. Middle-aged executives with brain tumors love it. Every day, Francine calls up and reads me another review."

I couldn't think of anything to say. I don't read many novels, and hadn't even heard of this one, so I told him about the unexploded bomb. He became excited and said he wanted to use it in his play. He said he liked the idea of people surrendering to reality. I couldn't get rid of him. He followed me until we got to Sarah's house, and he looked in the windows and said he had to go home and make a telephone call to New York. After he crossed the street I could still see his yellow hair through the fog.

For her party Sarah had borrowed a sofa from her old roommate, and most people were either on the sofa or in the kitchen. I had been to these parties before—these parties where everyone seems to have the same job except me. I was thinking that the only people who lived in London were writers and window dressers. Women were walking in and out of the room, talking about different designers. There were only two other men at the party, and they were talking to Sarah, who was leaning against the arm of the sofa. I hadn't seen any of the people there before but their eyes seemed fixed on me, as if they were acknowledging me, or as if they were looking right through me. I could hear music from the apartment above. It sounded like the English rock you never hear in America, the kind with a dead bounce and lyrics about unemployment.

The two men went into the kitchen, and then there were only women. One of them passed me a plate of food, letting her arm brush against mine. Another wanted to imagine herself in a dress of Sarah's, and looked down at her body after raising the hanger up to her chin. I was suddenly introduced.

But what could I have said to them? Should I have told them about Francine and her guinea pigs, or Leonard and his rats? Should I have told them about baseball—about Americans in London playing baseball?

They were curious about America. They asked questions and I tried to be of use. What's it like? Is it anything like *Dallas* or *Dynasty*? Is it like *Death Wish*? I started to tell them about where I grew up, about Midwestern suburbs. Then I told them about Midwestern cities and the vicious circle of crime and poverty. One of them said, as she leaned back into the sofa, "Oh, I didn't mean *that*. I meant something really rather different."

As they began speaking with each other, their accents became more musical. I didn't think they would ask me anything else then—about America or television, or about myself—and I didn't wonder what I would say if they did. The windows were open, and I looked out onto the sprinkled street. I could feel the wet, cold breeze move across my face, and could almost feel it move across their faces, in through their hair, until there was nothing left but breeze.

Everything was strange in that room, just as everything is strange in this city. A different world. Francine said I should treat London as an undiscovered treasure, that I should look for the gold buried in the ruins. I try to feel that way, but I know I never will. I just think of it as the place for me in this part of my life. Most of the time I feel like Bill and Fred. We linger, above the surface, as if we've just come up for air.

Apart

Robert is telling Schmuli about the high crime rate in the neighborhood, but I don't think Schmuli understands. Neither of them lives here. Robert's girlfriend, Laura, is my roommate, and Schmuli came a few days ago because he knows a friend of Laura's. They are both smoking the Israeli cigarettes that Schmuli brought with him from Israel. Robert wants to hear a story about the neighborhood or about the apartment building. "Yesterday, waiting for the subway," I tell them, "I saw a man blow his nose and then shine his shoes with the Kleenex." Robert nods. Schmuli says, smiling, "Kleenex?"

Robert likes to call his friends long distance and tell

them that we're the only white people in the building. It's not true. It was true when we first moved in, but now there are white people from New Orleans living on the eighth floor, and girls from Manhattan living on the fifth floor. The building is across the street from the Brooklyn Museum, and everyone is Haitian. There is a Haitian doctor living here, and a Haitian acupuncturist; we have a Haitian doorman, who is always reading a copy of the Haiti *Observateur*, and a Haitian restaurant around the corner serving goat curry. When you go to the grocery store, little black children, who I don't think are Haitian, bag white people's groceries—never black people's—then stare up and wait for money. Past the grocery store, there are abandoned brownstones, and I've read about tailpipe bombings, but I really don't know very much about the neighborhood. Robert does. He has been here only three weeks, and he knows more than Laura and I do. He is always asking questions, or telling stories about experts he knows. He has just come back from Europe, where he met a beer expert in Scotland, a blacksmith in Wales, and a sheep shearer from Australia on a train through Norway. One day he went to the hardware store and met a man who told him that Haitians are insulted when you call their language "patois."

The grocery store and the hardware store are on

Washington Avenue, and if you keep walking past the hardware store, it looks as if you could walk straight into the middle of Manhattan. From Laura's bedroom window, you can see the Citicorp Building.

I first saw this place on Christmas Eve. I was terrified because I thought I was probably going to be attacked, and because I didn't know what I was doing in New York. Laura and I had made an arrangement that she would fly out first and find a place to live. "Come out as soon as you can," she said on the phone the day she signed the lease. "It'll be great to have a man here." I thought she was joking, because that is exactly the kind of thing Laura jokes about, but when I saw the neighborhood, and the building, I realized she had been trying to warn me. It was Christmas Eve, and I just sat in the apartment, with no TV and no stereo, writing résumés, afraid to go out and buy a soda. Now, a year later, I feel perfectly fine on Washington Avenue, or on Lincoln Place, where the houses are gutted and someone is always selling drugs in the basements.

Schmuli, according to Laura, is afraid of the neighborhood. He hasn't told her this, but since coming here he has spent most of his time in the living room listening to music. Schmuli has been traveling across America, and he keeps his tapes in a suitcase and his clothes in a shopping bag from a record store. Every fifteen minutes he jumps off the couch and asks if he can change tapes, then he spends another fifteen minutes trying to find the one he wants in his suitcase. Laura says she knows it's the neighborhood: Schmuli wasn't always this way, she says. She spent a lot of time with friends of Schmuli's when she lived in Jerusalem.

Laura went to live in Israel after college, and before that, worked at Jewish camps for nine summers. She knows people all over the country, and sometimes, it seems, all over the world. Most of them are like us, Jews in their twenties who aren't sure what to do with themselves, or people like Schmuli who want to come to New York and stay with us. Laura has had six jobs in the last year, and she often talks about moving to California, where her uncle produces television shows. Last week, she heard about a graduate program in California in Jewish Family Recreation, which sounded to me like getting a master's degree in camp counseling. Robert wants to direct television shows and lately has been trying to persuade Laura to move to California so he can meet her uncle. Schmuli was in the army before coming here to travel. I work the second shift at an investment bank, doing word processing.

All the word processors at the bank are brilliant. They all have lapsed Ph.D. candidacies in Botany, or

Comparative Literature, or History of Science. We're supposed to work until two, but after midnight—after all the investment bankers have left—someone usually brings out a joint or a bottle of vodka. After one, we can take our vouchers to a woman on the ground floor and get cash for cab fare, which they're supposed to give us because the subway is unsafe at two in the morning. I can't think of anyone who actually uses the money for cab fare. If you never got your Ph.D. in History of Science, and you have to be a word processor, and you are probably earning more money than if you actually had the degree, chances are you're not afraid of subways.

My first job in New York was at a health-insurance company Xeroxing health-insurance claims. Every day, I would get a number that placed me in a certain category of ailments. Tens were gastro-intestinal; thirties were gynecological; seventies were psychiatric. I almost have a master's degree in art history, and when I daydreamed I would imagine the women I worked with as subjects of famous paintings. I spent my last few days there not Xeroxing at all, but turning an exceptionally tall woman working with a pile of pediatric claims into Parmigianino's "Madonna with the Long Neck."

Laura works as a waitress in Tribeca every night except Monday, in a restaurant owned by three Palestinians from Bethlehem. She went to Israel, she said, because she believed in Zionism. In Israel, she dated a Palestinian, learned Arabic, and doubted Zionism. When she returned, and was living with her parents, she became a Zionist again. Here in New York she doesn't know what she thinks. I know she wants to discuss Israeli politics with Schmuli, but she can't while Robert is around, because he never learned about the Palestinian.

Laura and I like to laugh at the Jewish radio station. They're always playing ridiculous things like "Seventy-six Trombones" sung in Yiddish or songs about Jews in Montana called "Come 'Round Again, Minyan Man." In New York we think of ourselves as people from Detroit, but in Detroit we always thought of ourselves as Jews.

Laura had a lot more to do with Jewish things than I did. She was always trying to get me to run for an office in our temple youth group, or go out with some girl who was president of the East Lansing chapter of some other kind of group. I never did. I always felt sorry for Laura because she hated high school so much, and never really got along with her parents. Now she feels sorry for me because she gets all the mail.

Laura, Robert, and I have known each other since we were little, and for the past few weeks we have spent most of our time talking about Detroit. It's no different with the people from New Orleans. The night they invited me upstairs, I was the only person who wasn't from New Orleans. They talked about parties and houses and drank Ramos gin fizzes and brandy milk punches. A girl there, who was up visiting for the weekend, told stories about her family. After each story, she said, "Isn't that so uptown New Orleans?" Everyone was drunk, but polite, so they asked over and over if I had ever been to New Orleans, and when I said no, they would try to change the subject for about five minutes.

Before I came to New York, I was supposed to work for an English-language newspaper in São Paulo. I'd met this Brazilian woman in graduate school named Else. Her mother was black and her father was a German Jew. I used the money from my loan to fly down. We lived together in a suburb of São Paulo, and everywhere there were peeling skyscrapers, vacant lots, and old cars. I tell people now that São Paulo looked like an overpopulated downtown Detroit. The newspaper job didn't work out, because they went broke the month after I got there, and Else and I fought all the time, mostly about money. Then Laura wrote to say she was moving to New York, so I said goodbye to Else and stayed with my parents before coming here.

In New York, except for our jobs, Laura and I practically never leave Brooklyn, and usually not even our neighborhood. Last month, though, my college roommate's mother, who lives in Manhattan, invited me to a party. My college roommate wasn't there, and I was the youngest person by about ten years. It must have been planned that way. All the guests seemed spaced out in ages, from me to someone in his eighties. I stood alone and drank champagne until a woman in her thirties asked me what I did. Then she apologized. Then she wanted to talk about people asking each other what they do. Did I think it was unfair, she wanted to know.

"I'm not sure," I said. "What do you do?"

She was a fund raiser for medical schools, which I told her sounded complicated. A man in his forties, who had been listening, told a story about riding a motorcycle on LSD and crashing into some famous rose bushes. Later, a man in his sixties talked about working in live television. A woman in her seventies, born in Vienna, said she spent the war hiding in a forest.

I had to talk about my neighborhood because my college roommate's mother told a group of people where I lived. "Oh!" said a man. "Eastern Parkway is the Fifth Avenue of Brooklyn."

The party was on Fifth Avenue. He and I walked out onto the terrace. We stood in the night air, discussing the architecture and demography of Eastern Parkway as though it were some sort of continuation of where we were—of the party, of the apartment; as though I were some sort of continuation of him.

I drank and drank champagne and imagined the caterers handing out cab vouchers. I took a cab back to Brooklyn, which cost me eighteen dollars. I didn't have enough money to buy pot, and Laura was working late, so I had to scrape out resin from the pipes and smoke that.

Since Robert has been here, he has bought all the drugs. He likes to describe the differences between European and American drug etiquette. Last night he rolled joints the way they do in Amsterdam, then the way they do in Madrid. He told us that in Madrid he was living in an apartment where the previous tenants had been heroin addicts, and there was blood on the walls. He said nothing like that could happen in New York; the landlord, he said, would paint everything over. Just as we were about to check the time, Laura walked through the door, so we knew it was after three. She said she wanted to go right to sleep and asked if there was any pot left. There wasn't because I hadn't worked that night, and Robert and I had smoked it all. Robert followed her into the bedroom, and I was left alone with Schmuli.

I didn't think I should say much to Schmuli. I knew

he didn't want to talk about being in the army and being in Lebanon, or his trip across America, or listen to stories about New York City. And I disagreed with Laura about why he stayed in the apartment—he seemed more tired than afraid to me.

The tape ended, and I pointed at the stereo. "What do you want to hear?" I said. He looked uncomfortable. I should have said something more. I should have told him what I was thinking: that all of us— Robert, Laura, Schmuli, myself—we're all the same.

Laura, Robert, and I were born in the same suburb in the same year, but ended up in different suburbs. Robert's from West Bloomfield; Laura's from Birmingham; I stayed in Southfield. We went to different high schools and different colleges, then traveled to different parts of the world. Schmuli was born a year after us, in Iran, and lived with his mother in Haifa before entering the army. But right now, we are all here, together, in this apartment.

Robert came out of Laura's bedroom and asked Schmuli to go with him to Lincoln Place. "Ever bought drugs in a basement?" Robert said. Schmuli smiled, and I didn't think he understood. I could hear Laura adjusting the shower water.

"He wants you to go, too," I said.

I got up with Schmuli and locked the door after they left. Laura was singing in the bathroom with her

waterproof radio. I pulled at the front door a few times
to make sure it was locked, then I walked to the window near the couch.

I couldn't see any tree trunks on Eastern Parkway,
only the branches, which looked woven together, and
I remembered a painting I had had to write about in
school, of Penelope, the woman in Greek mythology
who undid her tapestry each evening. Of course, here
it was just the opposite—everything staying woven in
the dark, until it's daylight, and the pavement shows
through.

Robert and Schmuli came back fifteen minutes
later, and we stayed up until nine. I wanted to clear
my mind before going to sleep this morning, so I
thought about last night. On the way to my room I
looked out the window at the trees, which were now
staggered, and I looked at them as though something—in a place I couldn't yet find—was touching.

Words

On the street I saw a woman I hadn't seen for years, a woman from high school. Between high school and the day I ran into her she had married and divorced two men, traveled all over the world, and served as a foreign correspondent in Beijing. In high school we were in the same production of *Alice in Wonderland*: I was Alice; she was the Cheshire Cat. That day on the street, as we chatted about her marriages and about Beijing, she grinned and I twirled my long blond hair. The whole exchange—the chatting, the grinning, the twirling—made us both seem doomed.

Another friend from school, someone for whom

doom is less of a diversion and more of a career choice, works with abused children. At one time she worked in a housing project populated almost exclusively by Laotian hill people. They were gracious and hard-working, but on occasion the men would throw the women and children down the stairs. My friend had a theory: In the hills of Laos, the ground is sufficiently soft, and the Laotian hill people are sufficiently short, so that being thrown out of one's hut (my friend's equivalent to being thrown down stairs in a housing project) was not only harmless, it was possibly affectionate. But the city, armed with statistical evidence, was not appeased by my friend or her theory. She was transferred to another city office, where she works with babies abandoned in subway cars or vacant lots or elevator shafts; where she makes more money, and the cruelty is beyond dispute; where it's the theories that are the diversions.

The man I live with has no use for me. (That's my theory.) But he anticipates becoming the marrying kind. He is a music critic for a weekly newspaper, and a frustrated everything: frustrated novelist, frustrated athlete, frustrated musician, frustrated husband. Doing any of those things to something nearing completion wouldn't help; it would only make him feel like a failed novelist, failed husband, and so on. The man I live with only notices things that don't matter, things he can live without.

Technically, he is a successful music critic; that is, people take him seriously in print. His theories of music criticism—kept secret, then revealed and reveled in—are to plagiarize George Bernard Shaw and to alliterate whenever possible. That's what David is all about: polished dishonesty and shallow wit. Last month, at three in the morning, a woman called up on the telephone and began to scream at me. She accused David of "sadism" in one of his reviews. She claimed that her husband—the aggrieved soloist— wouldn't talk to anyone; he wouldn't talk to her. I could hear a baby crying in the background. David, who was sleeping one of his sound sleeps, woke up and, after realizing what was going on, pulled the plug out of the wall. I wanted to ask him then what he had written and why he had written it. "Saccharine," I imagined him saying. "Sibelius. Get it?" David claims to admire honesty as a matter of fashion, but during a crisis it's his only excuse.

The other night, at a restaurant where the people at the next table were Jamaican and drunk, David's conversation with me came around to honesty. The husband kept ordering Tom Collinses in a heavy accent, after waving down the waiter with both arms. Each time he sounded as if he were saying, "Another Tony came in. Another Tony came in, if you please." David took the opportunity to tell me about a man at the paper whose wife decided to have her tubes tied behind her husband's back and then explained away the scar as a pencil poke: She told him about the "accident," he was fittingly concerned, things went back to normal. Several months later she overheard him talking on the telephone, exposing to someone her pencil-poking alibi. David told the story over and over, shifting sympathies, scrutinizing details. What was the likelihood of a pencil poking its way through a woman's blouse, then her abdomen, and making a scar similar to the one from this type of procedure? Did the husband's duplicity rest in not confronting his wife with her lie, or in using the lie to amuse his friends? And what about revenge?

I watched the Jamaican woman try to clean up after her baby. The baby's diaper was dripping; its pacifier was rolling around on the floor; its parents, for most of the evening, hadn't been interested. Suddenly, though, the mother began to notice her baby's discomforts, and without leaving the table, she tried to put things back into order. Eventually, after she had done all she could, she made her way to the bathroom unembarrassed as the baby leaked a neat trail through the restaurant. After his wife had gone, the husband ate the garnish off her plate and finished her Tom

Collins. He cleaned his shoes, then the area around his shoes, and ordered two more drinks. At first my sympathies had been with the baby, then the mother, but finally, as I watched the husband attract stares for both his selfishness and his drunkenness, he won me over.

I often threaten to do something specific, like work with abused children, or go back to school; the foreign correspondent wanted to know about my acting career. In the past six months, I have taken a test to get into law school, a test to get into graduate school, auditioned for a famous acting class, and missed the civil service exam three times. At the law-school exam, there was a false sense of camaraderie. At the graduate-school exam, everyone looked hated and pale. At the audition, in front of a panel of middle-aged men, I read a monologue of my own composition about a middle-aged man, called "Requiem for a Music Critic." The largest and hairiest of the middle-aged men thanked me the most appropriately and then suggested I become a playwright.

To take my mind off specific things, like leaving him, David has planned trips on our behalf. The first, last year, was to my parents' house. Then it was to Maine, where we first met. Then it was to England, where I had always wanted to go. David paid for everything, disguising each trip as an act of kindness, and it wasn't until later that I saw the shape of the conspiracy.

My parents had always liked David: his occasional letters, his phone etiquette, his ability to be entertaining but occupied whenever they came for a visit. But our stay at their house—David's first—was a conceded failure. David used my parents as easy targets, and they silently thought him a monster.

In recent years my mother took Valium and watched a lot of television, until she discovered bridge tournaments. Now she travels all around the Great Lakes, playing in tournaments, collecting master points, hoping one day to become a master. My father, for as long as I can remember, read the sports page and watched sports on television. Now, to pass the time while my mother is away, he has begun to read biographies and autobiographies of famous professional athletes. In a way, if you're David, my parents are easy targets, but someone should give them credit, if only for the lurch forward.

At first David talked about bridge with my mother and about baseball with my father. Everything was fine. One afternoon, though, I discovered him in their bedroom, looking through their things. On my mother's nightstand, he had found expired Valium prescriptions and a pamphlet entitled *The Weak Two-Bid*. On my father's nightstand, he had found several back issues of *Sporting News*. David held up an eight-year-old issue with rings from a coffee mug and said, "Your parents are fossils. You know that."

David refused to call me Sheila. He insisted on calling me Shelley, or Sheil. It made my father wince, and I think it's what compelled my mother to pull out the old clippings of my starring roles. We left two days early.

The day we returned from Maine—a trip shortened from a week to a weekend—David brought up the trip to England. He told me that he had invited the paper's book critic, a Peruvian Jew, over for dinner.

The Peruvian Jew had gone to school in England, but during dinner he would only talk about his mother. He hates his mother. He told us an intricate story, with asides, about the pair of stockings he sends to Peru each year for his mother's birthday. He kept a devilish smile on his face as he described the care he takes in camouflaging the gift (he has never used the same-size box twice), and his ritual ride to the post office in a taxicab. Later David had to explain: The Peruvian Jew's family is immensely rich, and his mother thinks of any anonymous package as a bomb.

The Peruvian Jew and David briefly discussed David's writing. The Peruvian Jew told David that he was "articulate in print," but in person he was "hyperarticulate." Because of his politeness and because of his arrogance, David agreed, but I was left to brood. What might a hyperarticulate person be like? How would he converse with us merely articulate types? I decided that a truly hyperarticulate person, feeling confined by verbal and visual languages, would need something else, something mathematical, I imagined. I have since been getting a great deal of comfort from the idea of these hyperarticulate people using mathematical equations to describe the color of someone's clothes, or the flavors in their dinner, or what they did that day last week when it rained.

Our trip to England was extended but unspontaneous. David, whose sense of humor can be both silly and cruel, began to use an English accent, as a joke, at first, then, I think, for sport. He insisted we loiter in unimportant, uninteresting places. We spent the last two weeks on a stud farm owned by a school friend of the Peruvian Jew. The friend was gone, and David and I stayed in the huge house alone. The house had columns and a great esplanade, and David and I began to play an elaborate joke, pretending to be Southern. He used a Southern Accent, and I made mint juleps with fresh mint and scotch whiskey. In the afternoons David would ride the horses, and I would go into one of the nearby towns.

In a town called Tring, there was a museum which the people from Tring called "the stuffed-animal museum." For days I stayed away from the stuffed-animal museum. I had expectations: case after case of century-old teddy bears; contemporary pink elephants; large zebras, their eyes made of ebony, their tails made of human hair, from Bedlam perhaps.

The stuffed-animal museum was not a toy museum but a taxidermy museum, with case after case of stuffed, occasionally lifelike birds. David, who has subsequently read about Victorian toys and taxidermy, walked through the museum the day we went with an entertained gait, wondering out loud.

The last few days on the stud farm someone called "the stud manager" appeared. His first day I sat watching him. He looked beautiful and wise, with the face of an old man and the body of a teenager. The afternoon before we left I went up to his small attic room above the stables and suggested we share the last of my whiskey.

I soon found out that the stud manager was neither beautiful nor wise. He had the teenager's predictable sadnesses and the old man's dreary habits. His smile was toothless. He blushed, then quivered. Finally, I said something. "Tell me," I said, "what exactly is it about horses that you love so much?"

"It's not just horses," he said, stuttering, possibly offended. "It's pigeons. And whippets. Anything you can race." He told me that he raced pigeons and showed me his boldface mention in *Racing Pigeon Pictorial*, then he went to a drawer and found pictures of his favorite pigeons. "I make them go as fast as they can," he said.

From the window I could see David on a horse, riding in a large circle, seeming part of some invisible carousel. There was a sobered smile on his face, as if he were getting somewhere, as if he couldn't see the large circle of his path, as I could.

The stud manager tried to regain my attention by offering the rest of the whiskey in his glass. Then he asked about "the friends back home," although I supposed he meant David.

"When I was in school," I said hurriedly, in deference to the stud manager's love of speed, and in despair of the remoteness of my own past, "everyone I knew wanted to be a doctor, or a psychiatrist, or an actress. Now I seem to know a large number of podiatrists, social workers, and wives. Under the circumstances, it is practically impossible not to think of life as merely a process of diminishment. Like irrational numbers. They just keep going and going. But to write one on paper—to understand one—you'd have to do something, wouldn't you? You would have to round up, or round down. You would have to make it stop."

I was drunk, and glib, and no longer seductive. But what I meant, what I wanted to explain to the stud manager, was that in the lives of those people he had accidentally asked about there are sudden and over-whelming desires to slow down—to stop, if necessary—before everything changes into something else, something different, unrecognizable, and lost.

But I was drunk. David was outside, spinning and spinning. My thoughts were too precise for words. And the man—the man whose room I was in, the man with the ancient face and ageless body—wanted things to go as fast as they could. It was late in the afternoon, and none of us was seeming quite human.

Eleanor in the Underworld

Eleanor oppresses her husband, Martin, with tiny gestures: driving dangerously, dropping the dinner, turning on the dishwasher while he is in the shower. Eleanor, who sleeps poorly, often wanders around the house until all hours, dazed but determined, knocking over picture frames and stacks of books. Alone in his empty bed, Martin must wake to go help Eleanor clear away the the broken glass, stepped-on records, shattered appliances. Eleanor—a guilty woman who feels no guilt—will end up back in bed with Martin. They will hold each other then in the familiar darkness, while Eleanor, silently amused, thinks of a recently departed coffee grinder, of the cracked photo-graph of Martin's sister's children.

Martin produces instructional videos for large cor-porations, small shows for prospective employees all about company policies and company morals—lurid technology and human folly reduced to a five-minute color display. Martin is a condenser by trade and by temperament; Eleanor reads in the living room.

Her hair is very dark now, and it curls gently, but unmistakably, with the shape of her face. Her fingers are long and dangerous-looking, stiff on the armrest of the sofa, or held, straight up, next to her sunken eyes. Her small lips, purple from drinking fruit juices and red wine, don't look like lips: They are thin and ir-regular, and she has a habit of turning them under her front teeth. Eleanor's smile is a horizontal crack, a lingering line, a mistake.

When it comes to getting through the day, Eleanor doesn't mix herself up with method. She is a woman of habit and can't bother with ideologies or analytic mod-els. When she cooks, and she cooks frequently, she refuses to consult pictures of the finished product shining up at her from the cookbook. She is a woman of hidden talents, indolent but contemplative, and, according to her own diagnosis, a survivalist at heart.

Martin is not like Eleanor. He is faithful, and he is a systematic investigator—of simplicity, in Eleanor's case. When they first met, Martin found something simple in Eleanor's looks, lots of primary colors and geometric shapes—red lips, blue eyes, yellow hair; the body as a series of soft, narrow ellipses. Eleanor doesn't think of herself that way at all, not in the least little bit. She looks in the mirror, or at old photographs, and sees something shapeless and spoiled, and certainly not pure. "Melted snow," she will think out loud.

Eleanor read too many books at an early age and considers herself the antiheroine of her own life. She injures without provocation, repeats terrible and fantastic lies, is known for lapses in taste and tact. Eleanor's wit is a scythe. She charges into rooms, indestructible, aiming just above the collar.

Sometimes Eleanor lives in a dream world. She dreams that she only imagines herself a fiend. Her cruelties become accidental; her kindnesses appear styled and significant. She becomes her dream: an old bone, a cream puff, another upholstered chair. "Poor inanimate Eleanor!" she tells herself. "She has lost the battle with propriety before it could even begin."

Eleanor doesn't mind very much—these gaps between her actions and her inventions, her imagined inability to do harm. She occupies herself with Martin and his thin good looks, his long neck, his apparent clairvoyance. Martin—sharp-featured, self-satisfied—

knows exactly what's coming next. He isn't ever surprised. Occasionally Eleanor wonders why: "It must have something to do with his neck," she once decided. (Martin's neck is long and complicated, faintly aristocratic; his head is far away from the ground.) Then she decided it had everything to do with etiquette, with the fact that Martin has an Attic politeness. "Martin is too polite to act surprised," she once told herself.

Martin believes his politeness is contagious. He actually believes that Eleanor's recent nocturnal "accidents" are in fact accidents, that she is trying to be polite by not turning on the lights during her pilgrimages to the kitchen, her sojourns in the bathroom. The idea that Eleanor might be picking up the coffee grinder, or the picture frame, or the magazine rack, and just throwing it on the floor doesn't enter Martin's mind. "Fool," Eleanor thinks, as Martin lumbers through the hall, scratching his blond stubble.

Sometimes Eleanor dreams about ways to change: She dreams of writing her autobiography. The book will be episodic, but coherent, in its documentation of insults, sporadic violence, sexual and gastronomic excesses, elaborate property crimes, orchestrated public humiliations. Eleanor, the grand intruder! And the book will end—as her life seems to be ending—with an undramatic acquittal. Eleanor is looking forward to that ending. She loves anticlimaxes.

Martin has his own suggestions. He believes that Eleanor needs inspiration from other people, just as he himself is inspired by other people. Martin finds crowds healing; the din of a crowd's voice is a symphony. Martin, intruding dramatically, with the will of an aristocrat, wants Eleanor to take people out from under the microscope, to stop looking at those specks from inside the plane window. Eleanor laughs at Martin's suggestions. "Ha!" thinks Eleanor, lying on the floor with her feet up on the sofa. "Ha!" she has actually said out loud.

Not that Eleanor isn't equipped for those sorts of endeavors: Eleanor knows quite a number of people, quite a number of men and women; so many, in fact, that it's difficult to tell them apart.

The women, of various ages and sizes, all believe in a world that goes down and comes around. They gain and lose weight, fall in and out of love with their husbands, go to work, have a child, back to work, another child. Eleanor isn't comforted by these women and their sundry exuberances, the way they give birth in between trips to the office. She looks at them and thinks, "The only tragedy is the tragedy of repetition." Eleanor flies through her life, as if she were riding a rubberband.

The men, whom Eleanor spies upon in the streets and at parties, are often like Martin—acquiring and dispensing without expression. Eleanor listens to them, not believing a word, wondering if they perm their hair, or embezzle money, or cheat on their wives. Eleanor, who perms her hair, steals money from Martin's sister's purse, and cheats on her husband, smiles, then turns to walk away from them in midsentence.

Actually, Eleanor hasn't done any of those things. The hairdresser, his voice shaking with pity, told Eleanor that her hair would never hold a perm. She took money from Martin's sister's purse at Martin's sister's suggestion; Martin's sister, busy holding a daughter, wanted to give the carryout boy a tip. And Eleanor is too busy fending off Martin's advances to think about anyone else. At parties, while the husbands mention their salaries or complain about their wives' insomnia, Eleanor looks at people's shoes, or finds things on the walls. Sometimes the husbands try conversation. They explain whatever with lengthened smiles and breathy laughter. Soon enough, though, they tire of Eleanor's absent expressions, her colorless hair, her many glances above and behind their faces. Then—as if she can read their minds—she will announce a wave of thirst, a fit of hunger. Eleanor backs up into kitchens, leaving men to fend for themselves, or return to their roundabout, renovated wives.

When she first met Martin, Eleanor believed in love. She believed that love—like music—could have a kind of precision. Now, from the window, Eleanor sees these men leaving home in the morning, or dragging themselves back at night, and she assumes they are leading loveless lives. Eleanor, sprawling out on the living-room carpet, holding a magazine in front of the light, has written the book on loveless lives.

Eleanor in the afternoon. When Eleanor reads books that document previously undocumented atrocities, she likes to begin in the middle, with the photographs. The book in her lap is about the Silesian and Sudeten Germans. Backed out of Poland, hounded out of Bohemia, the Silesian and Sudeten Germans were forced to emigrate—after hundreds and hundreds of years, after an eternity—to a new part of the world, deep in the Germany that months before—a moment before—had left them behind for the Russians. It was the end of 1945, and all over people were wandering around the cold hell they had made for themselves; no one was happy to see the Silesian and Sudeten Germans. Eleanor, twenty-eight, childless, appliances in the garbage, reads about special concentration camps where these technically German refugees were detained, forced to wear felt swastikas, beaten, demoralized, ruined utterly, then sent packing to live in the rubble. Eleanor, who often eats while she reads, moves through the pages of lost faces like an explorer: insatiable.

Eleanor in the bedroom. Eleanor's husband, Martin, has placed his chin on her stomach and his eyes look like a constellation, far away and interpreted, ever present in the darkness.

Eleanor at the grocery store. The frozen-foods section is an obstacle course. Hello, hello, hello. Eleanor bends into the freezer and smiles as she takes custody of the final box of baby peas.

After the grocery store, Martin and Eleanor are walking to the car. Martin is walking ahead, certain of everything, of his bony good looks and his undetected adultery, and he glances over his shoulder at Eleanor just as her bag of groceries spreads out over the parking lot.

Eleanor in the parking lot. There have been hundreds and hundreds of years. Years litter the blacktop. Is Eleanor snapping back? Martin is a microbe, a speck: smaller and smaller and smaller. The long journey upward! Is it over?

Everywhere

The day the English archaeologist arrived at my hotel
he asked me where he could swim in the ocean. I
described the island's circumference for him, starting
with the natural harbor: The natural harbor, the public beaches, the topless beach, the nude beach, the
nude singles beach, the nude family beach, the deserted nude beach, a stretch of shoreline not acknowl-
edged as beach, the resorts' walled-in beaches, the
gay beach, the nude gay beach, more resorts, the
airport, the inactive volcano, the excavation site, a
long stretch of nothing, slums, the man-made harbor,
the telephone exchange, warehouses, the natural har-

bor. He asked about the deserted nude beach. I described the black volcanic sand and the hollowed-out cliffs behind, the nationalities of people I had seen, the only restaurant, which was Chinese and which I said I couldn't recommend. He told me I was wrong about the cliffs. Morphologically speaking, he said, this was a typical island, and hollowed-out cliffs wouldn't occur because for some time—since its birth, he had learned before leaving England—the island had been sinking. I am not a geologist, of course, and not an archaeologist (I went to the island on a whim), and after our meeting I couldn't walk under the cliffs at the deserted nude beach as if they were hallucinations, but he was probably right about the island. Everything was in dispute there, as if people were pushing it into the sea.

The disputes were various—economic, political, logistical, anthropological, comic, violent—but always seemed connected to the fact of the excavation. Some disputes had been caused by the excavation, some predated the excavation but had been aggravated by it, some concerned the excavation site and nothing else; there were petty disputes, discussed by everyone then promptly forgotten; there were abstract disputes which could have shaken up someone who hadn't heard about the excavation and knew nothing about the island. For instance, because of the decade-long influx of tourists and, more recently, of journalists, archaeologists, and tourists interested in the excavation site, the garage was increasing exponentially, and no one would agree where to put the new garbage dump. There were illegal currency exchanges in the hotel lobbies. The airport's new runway was too short. There was ethnic violence between Hindus and Muslims and economic violence between the Chinese and the Vietnamese. An Italian photographer, in need of a white coral brick wall for a fashion shoot, wanted to sandblast a hundred-year-old façade off a block of former slave quarters. Since its independence the island and another island across the channel had been fighting a cold war over fishing rights. The team of Belgian archaeologists presiding over the excavation had arbitrary rules for deciding who could visit the site, how long they could stay, and what they could see while they were there. And results of radiocarbon tests seemed to suggest that someone might have to rewrite the history of the island, the history of the archipelago, the history of the oceans, and the history of the peopling of the earth's land masses.

The English archaeologist liked keeping track of events, and one evening he listed the island's disputes for his wife in what sounded like a prearranged sequence. I happened to be part of the conversation and asked him about it afterward: Why, for instance, had he begun with fishing rights and stopped with the peopling of the earth's land masses? He said he hadn't considered the order beforehand, but, when he thought about it, he had to admit that he didn't really care for fish, and that he truly believed a tree hadn't fallen—and for that matter, he added, an island couldn't sink—unless someone was there to know it.

I came to the island knowing nothing, on a whim, although for funding purposes I had to disguise the whim as someone else's. After reading about the excavation in the newspapers, I asked a friend at a foundation about the possibility of a grant. I hadn't seen her in months and was just making conversation, but the prospect excited her, and the next day she came to my apartment to tell me that I would have a better chance if she proposed the idea as hers and then proposed a list of recipients with me at the top of the men's list; as a formality, she explained, the foundation would first have to offer the grant to a woman, and she asked for names of unqualified women, or women who I knew wouldn't be interested. She always called me after committee meetings, and I knew that I had been chosen weeks in advance, but it was easy acting surprised with the president of the foundation. He awarded me the wrong grant over lunch, and then, after realizing who I was, told me that he himself had suggested my name. "I have a special interest in your work," he said.

My work before the trip had consisted of unpub-
lished travel books and eight-millimeter documenta-
ries, but the money officially came from the
foundation's mixed-media fund, so I could have done
anything I wanted. Originally—when I knew
nothing—I had ambitions: I decided to bring along a
sixteen-millimeter camera, an eight-millimeter camera, a video camera, a regular camera, dozens of
lenses, and a tape recorder; I brought volumes of an
empty journal, a table-top computer, an archaeologist's handbook, an atlas, and an extra passport. During my first week I developed a routine. Each morning
I would carry equipment down to the harbor, stand on
the pier behind the Sinhalese slum, and wait to buy a
hydrofoil ticket. (The only way to the excavation site
was by hydrofoil.) In line, I would pick out a stranger,
or a group of strangers, befriend them, photograph
them, tape them, follow them to the excavation site,
write down what I thought about them, and spend the
evening in my room hoping for an idea. Eventually,
though, I stopped using the cameras, and then the
tape recorder; I set aside my journal; I rarely went to
the excavation site. I could feel my ambitions narrow
and spent most of the time talking to people at my
hotel.

Everyone at the hotel was part of a familylike cluster. The English archaeologist had a wife, who was
also an English archaeologist. There was a young les-

bian from Seattle and her girlfriend, who was middle-aged and Dutch. There was a Canadian woman of French, African, and Malay ancestry, born on the island, and staying—discreetly, she said, because she was at the hotel and not at her brother's house—with a French journalist, there to write about the excavation, and his son from an unhappy marriage. There were three Swiss college students, two men and a woman, planning a trip to Fiji, and a waiter from the Upper West Side of Manhattan who wanted to be a novelist and often paid for the students' dinners. The man who owned the hotel was from Athens, and each morning he brought a new young man unself-consciously to breakfast. And there was myself and the man from Montgomery, Alabama. He arrived as I did, knowing nothing, but eventually came up with conspiracy theories about the excavation; we would stay up late on the terrace alone with his evidence, until the teenager from Australia, who slept on the terrace and thought no one noticed, returned from wherever and took off his T-shirt to use as a pillow.

People at the hotel, after my ambitions narrowed, tried to find new uses for my time. One of the Swiss students began needing help with his camera. On the terrace after dinner, the Canadian woman, who came out to the terrace to despise East Indians, would try to interest me in island politics or in also despising East

Indians; "They beat their wives the way other people
beat their children," she would say. The owner of the
hotel decided I should read Greek poetry and gave
me an English translation of Cavafy with little circles
next to poems about young boys having sex with each
other. The waiter from New York was always
reading—Freud by the swimming pool, Kafka at the
beach, T. S. Eliot in the Polynesian restaurant—and
found the Cavafy poems on a table where I had left
them. He became interested in a poem called "The
City," which didn't sound like it had a circle on its
page. The poem, he said, perfectly described his
mood on the island, and he thought it should also
describe my mood after he found out that I also lived
in New York. "You will find no new lands," he would
repeat to me. "You will find no other seas. The city
will follow you." The woman from Seattle and her
Dutch girlfriend, who were listening one morning,
told him not to bother with Cavafy or Greeks in general, or Freud, or Eliot—they couldn't get their minds
off the fashion shoot. The Dutch woman took the opportunity to ask why I didn't seem to have strong
feelings: "You're an artist," she said to me. When she
and the woman from Seattle were talking about the
fashion shoot they liked to use the word "desecration,"
which made me think of the excavation site.

There were a series of incidents during my stay on

the island—mutilations, or desecrations, really, under the circumstances. Someone was going over to the excavation site while the archaeologists were asleep and doing things to the artifacts: Amulet-like objects were being smashed; a wooden thing, relatively intact for something twenty thousand years old, was also smashed and its pieces left in the tidewater; bones were reburied.

The archaeologist in charge of the excavation site didn't like discussing the mutilations. In his photographs (the well-known one showed him holding tiny skulls in both hands) he looked like an explorer from the last century, but in person, invoking various rules he had established, or dodging questions about the most recent mutilation, he resembled a very contemporary bureaucrat. The reason he refused to answer questions about the amulet-like objects, and the bones, and the wooden thing, is probably because neither he nor any of the other Belgians knew anything about them, except their age, which had been calculated in a laboratory back in Louvain. The official pamphlet about the excavation, authored by special copywriters from London and doubling as a multilingual advertisement for the Belgian brewery that paid for the printing costs, claimed that two percent of the findings had been classified as "sacred," one percent as "nonsacred," and ninety-seven percent had yet to be classified. "Unknowable" was the word one of the Belgians used; he was supposed to spend his evenings in the archaeologists' pavilion going over that day's discoveries, but he developed a fondness for the discothèque and the impromptu international dinners in the restaurants. At sunset, from my hotel-room window, I could see him arriving in the motorboat he had privately leased from the Belgian consulate. He had a weakness for champagne, which people bought for him by the bottle after finding out who he was, and he never returned until morning. He always left behind his key in the ignition.

A discussion about the mutilations led to controversy at my hotel. The Canadian woman, who had gone to school in Paris, told us that Belgians were notoriously clumsy and insisted the archaeologists themselves had dropped the artifacts, or stepped on them. The English archaeologist's wife blamed a visiting group of other, unnamed archaeologists who were known for resolutely opposing new versions of the archaeological record. "Stubbornness," she said, "often leads to sabotage." Gossip about the mutilations, argued the waiter, was the climax of everybody's day. The man from Alabama said he knew a publicity stunt when he saw one. The lesbian and her girlfriend didn't care about the excavation site, and neither, though for different reasons, did the owner of the hotel. No one paid attention to anyone else, not even after the screaming started.

I could never make up my mind. Sometimes the desecrations seemed like accidents, sometimes obstinacies, sometimes culminations; sometimes they seemed part of another, more important lie; sometimes they seemed never to have happened at all. But whatever I was believing at a particular moment, I knew that . . . well, that wooden thing for instance. Put it together with the other things that had been dug up and it suggested something, but on its own it meant nothing at all, until it was found hacked to pieces.

After the argument, the larger familylike cluster of everyone at the hotel began coming apart. The Swiss students left for Fiji the next day, and the waiter joined them a few days after that. The teenager from Australia left for another island further up the archipelago, where he said the women were better looking and the police would let him sleep on the beach. The English archaeologist's wife went back to England. The Canadian woman broke down, and she, the French journalist, and the French journalist's son moved to her brother's house in the hills above the town.

"It is entirely possible," I confessed to the man from Alabama the day before he left, although I didn't suppose he was listening, "that I know everything there is to know about these desecrations."

I knew who was going over to the excavation site, how he went there, where he stood, and how he hid himself from his own noise. I knew all about it: How could I not have known?

My apartment in New York, the taxicab, the airport . . . the airport, the taxicab, my apartment in New York. I always felt on the island that I had already left it, or that I hadn't yet arrived. Always at the very ends of the trip, but in truth, of course, I was everywhere, with my body and with my life. Everywhere, like someone watching his own soul.

I finally had a sense of it—this everywhereness—the night before my plane took off. The people remaining at the hotel were treating each other as strangers, and I decided to take a walk, as I had often done, by the dock where the Belgian always left his boat. I walked by a small restaurant and saw a woman I had never seen before, although she had the confused accent and skin color of people native to the island, so I had probably seen her several times; I had probably always seen her. She spoke in French, asked me to sit down, to drink with her, and jokingly asked to be taken away—into the water, I thought she said. It reminded me of the Cavafy poem about the ancient town waiting to be sacked by barbarians. The townspeople wait until they realize the barbarians will never show up, because there aren't any barbarians left; everyone—everywhere—is waiting. I was more tired than drunk but jumped over the thin rope that separated the restaurant from the street. I sat down, and I brought her back to my hotel, I did everything, though of course I was waiting for someone of my own.

It's Freezing Here in Milwaukee

Sometimes I am in excruciating pain—so excruciating that I can barely walk across the room. I prop my feet up on pillows to keep the pain away. It's very simple, really: The arches—the metatarsal arches of both my feet—are falling, and when I try to walk in any direction, or stand up, the bones of my toes throb, and my eyes begin to water. It's unbearable. My surgeon, the man who is supposed to operate on my falling arches, is in Italy, and I am waiting at my parents' house for him to get back. Every day I read the weather report in the newspaper: "Rome—84° F.," or "Rome—91° F." My surgeon is in Rome, and my parents live in Milwaukee.

I don't have to stay in bed all the time. I could go down to the family room and sit on the La-Z-Boy, or into the basement and sprawl out on our old sofa. Sometimes, in the afternoons, I go into my parents' bedroom and lie down on their king-size bed. The bedspread, which is frayed and colorless, smells like the kitchen. It's like lying down on a tablecloth.

The surgeon is supposed to be the best in the country for this kind of surgery, so I gave up my apartment, took a leave of absence from my job, and came home to see him at his suburban clinic. After my second visit, the nurse gave me some cork-and-leather inserts so I could get out of the house and do things.

The cork-and-leather inserts, which are too big and slip underneath the soles of my feet, remind me of portable oxygen tanks. When I was in high school, I had a summer job at a factory on the south side of Milwaukee. The factory made portable oxygen tanks for people with severe respiratory illnesses so they could leave their houses without passing out. The company liked using employees instead of models for their brochures, and I remember one of the vice-presidents coming around every July to choose people. He would take them to the parking lot, fit them each with an oxygen tank, then get the photographer to take pictures of them getting in and out of a company car. Somewhere, in some part of the house, there is a brochure with a picture of me and a caption reading, "It really helps!"

I have spent the last three years of my life working on the metropolitan staff of a newspaper in New York City. Outside, everything seemed to be falling apart, but inside, in the newsroom, everything was getting better and better: new carpeting, new display terminals, record-setting circulation. I was a copy aide for two years, which meant that I clipped other people's articles and answered the telephones. In September of last year, the deputy editor called me in and said, "Danny, we're going to make you election coverage coordinator." Later that day I officially became "election coverage coordinator," which meant that in early October I was supposed to call the telephone company and order the extra telephones.

This past winter, I was promoted to editorial aide and sent to the Westchester bureau. My job there was pretty similar: answering phones and clipping articles. But about twice a month they would let me write a brief for the "Westchester in Brief" column. Right before my arches collapsed, they sent me on my first story: a python had escaped from a veterinarian's office in Tarrytown and gotten itself caught in the engine of a nearby station wagon.

A few weeks after I was sent to Westchester, Sally-Ann arrived. She had been a reporter for a Dallas paper and had just been hired by the metro editor. Sally-Ann lied about everything: her age, her salary, where she went to college. And she used me as a personal slave. "Daniel!" she would scream. "I need that clip ASAP!" The bureau chief, who is twenty-five (a year younger than I am), had been working on an investigative story for ten months: something about cocaine smugglers and a Larchmont pizza parlor. When he discovered a link with a pizza parlor in Amarillo, Sally-Ann said, "Let me work on this story. Get the paper to send me to Texas. I know Amarillo. I covered the Panhandle."

Sally-Ann had to stay in Westchester and was only allowed to cover the municipal courts. One afternoon at the courthouse, she saw Tony Seligman. (Tony Seligman writes for the national desk and has a Pulitzer Prize.) Sally-Ann came back to the bureau and started asking questions. Why was Tony Seligman in Westchester? What had he been doing at the courthouse? Why couldn't someone have told her that Tony Seligman was doing a story at the courthouse? Sally-Ann became frantic and called up the national desk. "Hello, Tony?" she said. "This is Sally-Ann Hughes. Remember me? I work up at the Westchester bureau? I heard you were doing a story up here at the courthouse, and I thought that if you need any help perhaps we should meet and talk. I know the courthouse.

It's a pretty closed place without contacts." Tony Seligman didn't want to have lunch with Sally-Ann, and
he wasn't interested in meeting any of her contacts.
He was getting married in three days and had gone to
the courthouse to buy his marriage license.

On my last day of work, Sally-Ann came up to where
I was sitting and handed me a list of forty names. She
wanted me to find out the people's phone numbers,
and then call and invite them to her birthday party.
"Of course," she said, "I would have invited you, but
you'll be back in Idaho by then, won't you?" Most of
the people on the list had to be reminded of Sally-
Ann's last name before they remembered who she
was. Tony Seligman and his new wife were on the list,
but I couldn't get up enough nerve to call them.

When I went downtown to ask if I could have the
year off, the metro editor said, "Of course. We can't
afford to lose you. The year you were election coverage coordinator, everything went as smooth as silk." A
few times since I've been home, my father has bought
the national edition of the paper and left it on the
dining-room table as a surprise. I spend the afternoon
going through it as if I had never been inside a newsroom, and never lived in New York.

When I first moved to New York, I tried to get all
points of view. I tried and succeeded in befriending
the couple who lived across the hall. She had a ge-

netics degree from MIT, a law degree from Harvard, and a medical degree from Yale. Her husband used to joke that the only thing left was divinity school. The first time I saw her, she was pregnant and wearing high heels, and walking down the stairs as I was walking up. After the pains in my feet became worse and I could think of nothing but my own suffering, she gave me a list of five specialists: four in New York, and one in Milwaukee.

Their names were Carol and Ron Platt, and they often introduced me to their friends. One of the friends, a man from India with advanced degrees in mathematics and philosophy, would throw dinner parties in his small apartment and explain things using mathematical metaphors. He would begin: "There isn't a society, there isn't an individual consciousness, that doesn't start out believing it is getting closer to one, and farther from zero. We move, step by step, away from the latter and towards the former. But with each step our courage diminishes, and our steps become smaller. You see, we eventually realize—we sane ones—the infinity of numbers between zero and one. We realize that we have never been at zero, and we will never reach one. Our past remains a fiction and our future an impossibility." Then someone would ask him if he had ever been compared to Bertrand Russell, and he would say, "Of course, dear girl."

The summer before I was sent to Westchester, I slept with a woman who lived in the mathematician-philosopher's building—one of those giant fortresses on Second Avenue. It was August, and I was supposed to be on vacation. I couldn't afford to leave New York, and I went to a party with a copy aide from the foreign desk. It was hot and crowded, and I didn't know anyone except the copy aide. I remember a man of about thirty, slightly overweight, refusing to take off his suitcoat. He was surrounded by people who seemed to know him, and who seemed to be chanting, "Take it off! Take it off!" Someone had put bottles of wine underneath the air-conditioner to keep them cold. I took one of the open bottles and sat on the floor next to the window. I could see the copy aide looking around the room for me, then I could see him go into the hallway. Standing above me, leaning on the air-conditioner, was a woman in a green T-shirt and a long skirt. She moved closer, and the air-conditioner blew the hem of her skirt against my face. She was looking down at me, keeping her hair up in a bun with one hand, and holding a bottle of beer with the other. She seemed to be swaying back and forth, and I thought she might be drunk. As she came toward me, she let her hair fall down around her shoulders. She put the beer on the floor and ran her fingers across my forehead. "Hot?" she said. She had my head between her hands. "We'll have to make it go faster," she said, and tilted her head toward the air-conditioner. "We'll have to make it go as fast as it can!"

During the cab ride to her apartment, the driver stopped to buy cigarettes. She rolled down the window and started screaming. Then she opened the door and grabbed my hand, pulling me into the street. She kept saying she was a stockbroker and that she had had a really bad day in the market. "Really, really bad," she kept saying. "Really bad." As we walked the rest of the way, I decided to ask if she had lost her job, if she had been fired. "Really, really bad day," she said.

Her apartment was on the twenty-third floor, and it wasn't until I looked out the window that I realized the man from India lived a few floors below her. She turned on the air-conditioner and stood in front of it, holding her hair above her head again.

I decided she was either moving in or moving out. There were paintings stacked on the floor, a very large television set next to its box. She must have sensed my confusion because she walked away from the air-conditioner and kicked a pile of paintings. She kissed me on the mouth, and we stood in the hot darkness, taking each other's clothes off, waiting for the room to get cold.

In the middle of the night, I walked around the

apartment. There was a basket of unopened mail addressed to Judith Simms—her last name, I assumed, was Simms. In the bathroom, there was a bottle of French shampoo made from walnut leaves, and an unused bar of soap. I was hungry, and I went into the kitchen. She had two gallons of olive oil, an empty refrigerator, and empty cupboards.

The next morning, I woke up and she was sitting on the couch, wearing her green T-shirt. She wasn't wearing any underwear, and as I got out of bed, she put her hands in her lap. "I don't know what's the matter with me," she said. "I feel real sick. Do you?" I thought about staying and taking a shower with the walnut-leaves shampoo, but she seemed to want me to leave. "I have to get to work," I said, lying.

It was about seven-thirty. I stood in front of the elevator with two men and two women, all in suits. After five minutes, I decided to walk down. The stairs were wide and well-lit. I remember speeding down the stairs, flight after flight, talking to myself. I was sure I was the only person not waiting for the elevator. But I had overestimated my endurance, or underestimated how long twenty-three flights of stairs are. I got to the point where I was so dizzy and hot that I had to sit down. There was something awful about the situation—spending my vacation surrounded by stairs, running away from some girl I never wanted to see again. I leaned back against the concrete to catch my breath.

When I first moved to New York, I couldn't wait for anything: I could feel myself crackling inside. But it all changed. It must have changed because I fled New York the first chance that came along.

Here in Milwaukee, everything is beginning to freeze. Yesterday, my father took our cars in to have the snow tires put on; neighbors' yards are starting to look like tundra. I stare outside, and I can't help thinking about my surgeon. In Italy, they are having the hottest November in history. It's over one hundred degrees. People are passing out in the streets. I try to imagine what my surgeon is doing: Has he abandoned Rome and gone to the beach? Has he sacrificed his vacation to treat the heat-stroke victims? Or perhaps, like the Romans I saw on the evening news, he has given up and lain down in a fountain.

While I wait for him, I often lie in bed with my feet on the headboard. I follow the ceiling as it slopes down to the windows, then I look out to the backyard. When I was a child, we had a pear tree and an apple tree growing next to each other. In late summer, the ground would be covered with pale, green things; you could never tell whether they were apples or pears. From far away—from my bedroom, for instance—they all looked round and indisputably apples. From closer

up—the back porch or the driveway—they would become yellow and irregular, like hourglasses. Not until
you got on your hands and knees, or picked them
up—not until after that—could you possibly know for
sure.

My parents cut down the apple tree so they could
install central air-conditioning, and the pear tree has
stopped bearing fruit. Its leaves are all gray and
brittle.

In a way, nothing turns out to be what you think it
is. Sometimes the yard looks empty—it doesn't even
look familiar. But if I rushed outside, I could feel
those pear leaves, like wet sticks between my toes,
and know exactly where I was. And I could look up to
my bedroom window, just able to make out a corner of
the room, the place I'm looking at right now.

Leaving

David, a man I lived with and tried to abandon, decided that competence was a kind of genius. He gave up—and denounced—his job as a music critic in New York to take a teaching post in Los Angeles. "There is no difference between loving music and loving music well," he said; he imagined rooms full of eager average students. We were on the phone long distance when he told me. I had left him in New York (the abandonment) to attend law school in the Middle West. I had left our life together, and now he was leaving it too. I imagined two other people, another David, another Sheila, in our apartment, oblivious and bored respectively. "Maybe I'll come out for a visit," I told him. David's first apartment in Los Angeles was in the center of the city across the street from MacArthur Park. I arrived last month and have been staying farther west, in Hollywood, with Everett, my friend from law school, and, before he disappeared, Everett's boyfriend. Recently David told me (we speak on the phone instead of seeing each other; seeing each other, he claimed, would be "too powerful") that he is moving to Venice Beach. We seem to be playing leapfrog across the continent. His students are oblivious, I have concluded, hopeless: He wants to listen to the ocean from his bedroom window.

Everett and his boyfriend were like reactivated high school sweethearts. They did, in fact, attend high school together, but apparently never met until I met them, years later in law school. They would often bring up events—the Homecoming Dance of 1976, the afternoon when someone put real fish in the swimming pool, the sniper caught just in time behind the gymnasium—and imagine having seen one another across the crowd, in hallways, in locker rooms, in pizza parlors or in parking lots. After they arrived in Los Angeles, Everett liked to disappear with their car—to go sleep with someone else, he confided to me—and leave his boyfriend alone, or, after I arrived, with me, in their rented house. They bought the car to drive

across the country together. They were appalled by
Salt Lake City, appalled by Las Vegas; they amused
each other with theories about the kinds of people
who manage motels. (Everett kept me posted with
collect calls.) I flew out to Los Angeles and bought a
car on the way in from the airport—I asked the cab-
driver to drop me off at a used-car lot.

Everett's boyfriend often claimed to feel earth-
quakes. "Neighbors rearranging furniture," I once
heard Everett answer, though usually he said nothing.
Everett tells the same stories over and over, and one
night, while Everett was telling, again, the story of his
mother's friend's suicide, his boyfriend interrupted,
claiming for the second time that day to have felt an
earthquake. I thought of the famous Kleist story, "The
Earthquake in Chile," in which an earthquake inter-
rupts an imprisoned man's attempt at suicide: The
prison promptly collapses, and the prisoner, who has
been miraculously saved, escapes. Everett said nothing in response to his boyfriend and finished up his
story; I too—or so I imagined—had felt something,
and said nothing. The next morning, Everett's boyfriend was gone.

It is fall in Los Angeles, the season of hot dry winds
and spontaneous brush fires. Everett, after his boyfriend left, began to talk about the wind and the fires,
as if to say: How far could he go? He and his boyfriend

dropped out of law school in early summer, after exams, while all the administrative secretaries were on vacation. They wrote out separate, but identical, letters of resignation. I packed my things three weeks into the fall semester and called the Dean collect from the Los Angeles airport. He only remembered who I was when I told him I wasn't coming back. After his boyfriend had left, and before he started working, Everett and I would watch his neighbors, who possibly own their homes, water their lawns. By early evening everyone's grass was as lifeless as Everett's. (Everett claims not to water his lawn because of the drought and because he hasn't figured out where the hose is.) On the news we saw a story about a retiree who had decided to deep-soak his lawn while he went to the grocery store. His house overlooked the ocean, and, when he came back, his lawn, and the tons of earth underneath it, had collapsed onto a woman driving home from the beach. She was unharmed. "I was looking at my mascara in the rear-view mirror," she told the reporter. "And suddenly the mirror was in the back seat." Everett and I drove out to investigate the next morning. "They don't have weather in Los Angeles," said Everett, finishing up his third beer as we stopped for a red light on the Pacific Coast Highway. "Only wrath." He laughed and asked me to hold onto the steering wheel while he opened another beer. I told him to finish mine. I had had four already. We turned around at a barricade and never saw what we had seen on the news—hills of dirt on the road, the ledge of concrete where the man's lawn had been— and made it back to Everett's before noon. I spent the rest of the day applying salves and creams: The wind had taken all the moisture out of my lips, face, and cuticles. "Cuticles?" demanded Everett, before getting into his car and disappearing.

Of course I am not always staying at Everett's. Occasionally he sends me into the Hollywood Hills, to a mansion owned by a friend of his, who is actually away. There are other guests at the mansion: an immigration lawyer and her Salvadoran boyfriend ("He doesn't speak any English," she said to me, smiling. "Can you tell?"); a twenty-eight-year-old coed from UCLA; a stockbroker living in the guest house; the maid, who is actually taking the place of the real maid, and, though she is Mexican, is also named Sheila. Everett's friend is moving, and every day that I have been there men have come to remove things, usually carpets and enormous indoor trees. There is marijuana, to which the guests help themselves, kept in an antique cash register on top of the wet bar, and I have often spent days, instead of finding a place to live, smoking pot with Sheila the maid. The palm trees, all around the mansion, and below, between the buildings of Los Angeles and the mansion, are as awkward as ostriches.

Everett sounds ashamed when he asks me to go, and then less ashamed when he admits to wanting to bring men home to sleep with. He often takes me out for dinner. One night we went to a restaurant in the shopping center on the corner of La Cienega and Beverly Boulevard. I listened to Everett talk about the shopping center ("something out of a Godard movie"); his friend's mansion ("sounds like the setting for a Robert Altman movie"); the restaurant's decor ("William Cameron Menzies could have anticipated this place"); the street person in the parking complex ("That black man with the pastry bag on his head looked a klansman in *The Birth of a Nation*"). For dessert Everett and I split an order of fried green tea ice cream. "Where tempura meets ice cream," said Everett. He said there was a health food restaurant in Los Angeles called "I Love Juicy," and a radio program called "Morning Becomes Eclectic," and a gun store called "Gun Heaven." He often has to drive past the florist shop in the Orthodox Jewish neighborhood with the marquee that reads "Happy Yom Kippur!" After dinner we drove across the street to buy champagne. "Trying to leave a supermarket in Los Angeles," said Everett, "is like deciding when to get off the freeway." There were too many places to pay: cash-only lines, coupon lines, fifteen-items-or-less lines, inexplicably empty lines. Everett insisted on paying for the champagne because I couldn't stay at his house the night before, and because that morning my car had been towed.

It was Sheila's day off, and I had agreed to wake up at ten to let the gardeners in, and was considering going to see a realtor in West Hollywood. When I walked outside, my car was gone—stolen, I assumed. I called Everett, but he wasn't home. I called David and hung up when he answered the phone. I called my mother long distance. No answer. Finally, as an afterthought, it seemed, I called the police, who suggested that I come in to file a claim. The gardeners gave me a ride to the station. "You look disappointed," said a policeman after telling me that, according to the maid, my car had been blocking the driveway and had been towed and not stolen. He told me that I could walk to the tow-away garage and wrote out directions on a Jack in the Box napkin. "You can't miss it," he said. I missed it for an hour. I wandered around a part of Hollywood where there seemed to be nothing—no people, no cars, no buildings, only what looked like the remnants of the backs of buildings. ("It looks like a mews," said Everett, after I told him the street name. He said the neighborhood was famous for its male prostitutes.) When I reached the garage, a man without teeth, sitting behind plate glass and petting an Afghan hound, was helping an astonishingly attractive couple try to recall the color of their rented car. The male half of the couple grew bored and reached into his pocket for what looked like a tortilla. He crumpled the tortilla in his hand and then ate it, piece by piece. I thought of my plane ride out—how clear the weather had been, so clear that the land below had looked like a map, like the maps I had made in grade school, I decided in the tow-away garage, out of salted cookie dough—until the couple disappeared. The man without teeth took my hundred and twenty-nine dollars and told me where my car was. I drove back to Everett's friend's mansion and sat in the Jacuzzi until Everett picked me up for dinner.

I have, in looking for book stores, misread minimall marquees and found myself parked in front of box stores. There are innumerable box stores in Los Angeles, according to the immigration lawyer, because people are always moving. She, herself, often moves, back and forth between San Francisco and Los Angeles, then around Los Angeles, to Pasadena, to Manhattan beach. She is staying in the mansion, in the master bedroom, and not at her apartment because her current roommate, a Filipino man she used to date, is jealous of her new Salvadoran boyfriend. I had been wanting to read a Jean Rhys novel—it didn't matter which one. One night when I was staying at Everett's house, he called me up at two in the morning and asked if I could stay somewhere else. I got dressed and drove, although I had no intention of stopping, past David's apartment building. (His car wasn't there.) When I arrived at Everett's friend's mansion at four, Everett was in the library watching television. "Is the plural of gin and tonic 'gins and tonic'?" He was too drunk to notice that he had been watching a transmission signal. We got in my car and drove to the Fat Burger on Santa Monica Boulevard. "It's the end of the world," said Everett, "and we're ringside." Everett changed his mind about eating and I took him to his house, put him to sleep, and fell asleep myself on the sofa. The next morning, Everett was gone, and there was a *Complete Novels* of Jean Rhys with an inscription ("From One Intransigent Transient to Another") in the front seat of my car.

David, at least on the phone, and regardless of his students, is inspired in Los Angeles, particularly at night. (He cites Jean Baudrillard.) Among the things he understands, he says, as if for the first time, are jazz, television, America, and sex. I suspect, although do not accuse him, of seeing other women. (Why shouldn't he? I argue on his behalf: After all, I left him.) Soon after arriving, I got into the habit of driving past his apartment building at night to look at his empty parking space.

Having had three gins and no tonic, having just reread *Good Morning, Midnight*, having failed, twice, to understand the twenty-eight-year-old coed's major, I decided to drive near MacArthur Park, past David's apartment, the beautiful apartment in the terrible neighborhood ("like New York," he said) that I had never been inside of. It was two, or three, or four in the morning. The police stopped me blocks from his building. They made me stand on the pavement. "Recite the alphabet backwards from X," one of them said. I started with Z. "Touch your left hand to your nose." I used my right. I was put in handcuffs, with one handcuff attached to the police-car door handle, while someone got in my car and drove away. "Where were you going from?" one of them said. "Going *from?*" I giggled to myself. The police officer with the mustache and the hair transplant ("Did he look like a transsexual?" asked Everett, who often has problems with the police and never forgets a face) was staring at my driver's license, which still listed my parents' address—middle western, suburban. "Daisy Lane," he said. "In Mapledale." "Why would a pretty lady ever want to leave a pretty place like that?" They locked my hands behind my back and put me in the police car. At the police station I failed my breathalyzer test by one one-hundredth of a point and was arrested for driving under the influence. Under my influences, I thought, that's my problem. In my cell there was a sobbing Korean woman, and, eventually, a teen-ager. "It's not my day," I said to her, just after she sat down. "Girl, it ain't nobody's day." She was in for armed robbery. I could, of course, have called someone—Everett, the immigration lawyer, my mother, David, but it never occurred to me. I had stopped noticing the phone in the corner of the cell, and the odors (body odor, horse manure perhaps, cigarette smoke). In the morning, the teenager and the Korean woman, with dozens of men, were taken, in bright orange manacles, to another jail. I was alone.

"What was it *like?*"

David, for whom curiosity is the highest form of sympathy, wanted to know what I had thought jail was like. (Everett, and the immigration lawyer, of course, already knew.) "Like being underneath my life," I wanted to say. (I said nothing.) I didn't want to explain, however, about the relief of being away, of the particular darkness of the jail cell, of looking up and seeing my life as some kind of lit fortress, and pretending that it's my life that is the prison.

I was released, as the phrase goes, and told by a jailer not to drive my car—"Don't lie until you're sober," I thought she said. (In fact, my car had been impounded, taken to the garage in Hollywood, placed under the care of the man without teeth.) On the street, in the sunlight, I was stopping. The pavement was soft, doughy, beneath my feet, and ostrich feathers seemed to be covering the sun. I felt as if my imagination were swallowing me. At a phone booth, I called Sheila, the maid. She had been disconsolate after learning that the police had towed my car and not the immigration lawyer's, and she picked me up— gratefully, I remember thinking—near the Yum Yum Donut on Highland Avenue.

The day I got my car back David asked me to move out to Venice Beach. I will see him tomorrow for the first time, in our new apartment, where the front lawn is made out of sand. I resisted at first. I told him that the woman he had lived with in New York was another Sheila, that she was probably still there. "Oh, there's always been another Sheila," he said.

He was right, of course, about the other Sheila. It was the other Sheila who had been driving drunk, under her influences. The only thing I am guilty of, in the words of the judge, is "excess speed." My cousin's friend's friend, a lawyer from Woodland Hills, who estimated the ressale value of his house as we waited for my case to come before the court, had struck a bargain with the District Attorney's office. "I was a failure as a lawyer," I told David. "And now I am a failure as a criminal."

Today I drove out to Burbank to eat lunch with Everett. We ate in the commissary of the movie studio where he works. His job, he explained, is to read a book like Italo Calvino's *Italian Folktales* and suggest that it would make an unprofitable children's movie, unlike in New York, he said, before he went to law school, where his job was to read books like *The Secret Garden* and *Treasure Island* and decide that public television would turn them into overbudgeted miniseries. We reminisced about New York. (Everett and I lived in New York at the same time; we imagine having seen each other, greeted each other.) During lunch I noticed that many of the studio employees, in their awkwardness, in their sadness, looked like law students. How heavy we seemed, Everett and I, back where we began, but not exactly, as if all we could do in our lives was shift weight. We began to talk about Los Angeles and laugh. ("An easy target, Los Angeles," said Everett. "It's only virtue.") Everett told me about his boyfriend resurfacing in Seattle; I told him, finally, that I was moving in with David. And why shouldn't we stay in Los Angeles? (We were sober, allowed to lie.) You don't love your boyfriend; you are still in love with David. There was a sudden lightness, a grace, in our joking, in our rhetoric. We argued for the quickness of the heart and against the roundness of the world, as if it were love, or the lack of it, that had to do with falling off.

After lunch I drove through the mountains, to the

ocean, where I felt full of hope. I had gotten out of my car and was standing on the sand when I began to see them. Only surfers, of course, but I hadn't seen them going in; they seemed to have come from nowhere. I thought of the wild swans at Coole drifting on still water. (Though, of course, the surfers were speeding, and their water was a wall.) How light you are! I imagined. I thought of them as standing on waves, with no expression on their faces, nothing on their minds. How light, I thought, and guiltless. I decided that they could rise—were rising—above the light.

Outside of David's house, at night, on the sand, I will skid before the nighttime ocean, the inky stillness. Nothing happens on a beach during an earthquake, but then, and it must seem like a miracle, the big wave comes. Suddenly, finally, the shore is free.

A NOTE ON THE TYPE

This book was set in a digitized version of Caledonia, a Linotype face designed by W. A. Dwiggins (1880–1956). It belongs to the family of printing types called "modern face" by printers—a term used to mark the change in style of type letters that occurred about 1800. Caledonia borders on the general design of Scotch Roman, but is more freely drawn than that letter.

Composed by American–Stratford Graphic Services, Inc., Brattleboro, Vermont
Printed and bound by Fairfield Graphics, Fairfield, Pennsylvania
Designed by Anthea Lingeman